Claire expected Ethan to leave, but he didn't. The porch light glowed behind him, bathing his head in gold. He might have looked like an angel, except for the sinful amount of interest brewing in his eyes. She glanced away, worried the same might be visible in hers.

"Have you ever wondered how it might have been between us if we'd stayed married?" he asked.

The question caught her off guard. So much so that she answered with the unvarnished truth. "Can something that intense last?"

"Or does it burn itself out?"

She chanced a look at him now, and stoked up her courage enough to ask, "Have you reached any conclusions?"

"I used to think I had." He tugged at a lock of her hair before tucking it behind one ear. She thought he might kiss her—he'd leaned that close. But he stepped back instead. "Till tomorrow, Claire."

Dear Reader,

Journeys take many forms. For Claire Mayfield, what starts as a bicycle trip to raise money for exploited children turns into a quest to confront her past and forge a new future with Ethan Seaver, the man she'd married and quickly divorced a decade earlier.

For me, writing this book was a journey of sorts. I've always flown solo as a writer. I've never had critique partners, much less collaborated with other authors on a series of books. When the opportunity to write *Found: Her Long-Lost Husband*—the last book in the SECRETS WE KEEP trilogy—presented itself, however, it was simply too good to pass up. I got to work with Liz Fielding and Barbara Hannay, two talented and accomplished authors I've long admired.

As we brainstormed via e-mail to come up with the reasons all of our heroines embarked on their emotional journeys, I found myself challenged and inspired in countless ways. This experience has taught me that it's good to shake up the status quo every now and then and try new things.

I hope you enjoy Claire and Ethan's story.

Best wishes,

Jackie Braun

JACKIE BRAUN
Found: Her Long-Lost Husband

SecretsWeKeep

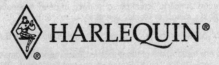

TORONTO • NEW YORK • LONDON
AMSTERDAM • PARIS • SYDNEY • HAMBURG
STOCKHOLM • ATHENS • TOKYO • MILAN • MADRID
PRAGUE • WARSAW • BUDAPEST • AUCKLAND

ISBN-13: 978-0-373-03982-1
ISBN-10:   0-373-03982-4

FOUND: HER LONG-LOST HUSBAND

First North American Publication 2007.

www.eHarlequin.com

Printed in U.S.A.

SecretsWeKeep

Share the love and laughter with three friends—
on their journey to wedded bliss....

Amid the breathtaking peaks of the Himalayas,
three women on the most challenging cycling
adventure of their lives are about to
share the secrets of their hearts.

They make a pact to change their lives.
And when the trip comes to an end, and the
three new friends head home to different corners
of the globe, Belle, Simone and Claire
start taking charge of their destinies....

Meet the men who will share their secrets and
bring love and laughter to the lives of these
extraordinary women.

First you met Belle, in
Reunited: Marriage in a Million

Last month you shared Simone's story,
Needed: Her Mr. Right

**And now, the unforgettable journey ends
with Claire, in**
Found: Her Long-Lost Husband

For my 10 sisters-in-law: Martha, Patti B., Izumi, Diana, Diane, Kathy, Barb, Judy, Patti H. and Holly. How did I get so lucky?

PROLOGUE

CLAIRE MAYFIELD STEPPED off the connecting flight in Chicago's O'Hare Airport on the last leg of her long journey home and breathed deeply. She'd been on airplanes and sitting in bustling terminals in various spots around the globe for the past twenty-some hours, having flown out of Hong Kong International Airport.

She was jet-lagged, hungry for real food and eager to soak away the grime of travel with a hot bath. She also needed to find a man.

Not just any man. Her ex-husband, Ethan Seaver.

Just thinking his name had the air backing up in her lungs. Nerves, she told herself, even as her body's reaction suggested something else. Claire ignored it, as she always did, exhaling slowly. Her reason for needing to find him had nothing to do with renewing their relationship, even if that were a possibility, which it wasn't. No, she didn't want to go back. She wanted to move forward. To do that, the past needed to be settled first.

As she made her way through the crowd of passengers, she switched the heavy carry-on case to the other shoulder. She was petite, fine-boned and just a hair over five-two in her stockinged feet, but for the first time in her life she had actual muscles defining her calves and thighs, and sculpting her shoulders and upper arms.

She had been away from Chicago for not quite three weeks, during which time she had bicycled four hundred kilometers through the Himalayas to raise money and awareness for the plight of exploited children. In many ways, though, it felt as if she'd been gone a lifetime. She was a changed woman—or at least a changing one. She felt stronger, more independent. She was determined to stand on her own two feet—this time for good.

In tackling the Himalayas on a twenty-one-speed bike, she'd begun another journey. This one was about self-discovery and, just as in the mountains, she had traveling companions for this trip too—Belle Davenport and Simone Gray. They made an unlikely trio—an American, a Brit and an Aussie who'd seemed to have little in common except for their gender and their obvious lack of athletic prowess. They were determined, though. Each had had something to prove—to themselves and to the people who looked at their seemingly cushy lives and sold them short.

They also had secrets. Secrets they had shared with no one until sitting in a tent high in the mountains, hands blistered, knees scraped, backs and behinds ridiculously sore, they'd exposed wounds far more damaging. Wounds that had festered for years.

In Belle's case her seemingly perfect marriage was a sham, her well-heeled life a lovely façade intended to conceal an ugly childhood that had seen her and her young sister relegated to foster care and only one of them adopted. It hadn't been Belle. She'd been forced to scrape and claw her way to adulthood on her own, where she'd become a successful morning television personality. Now Belle was determined to leave her husband and find her sister, Daisy.

Simone's secret was equally heartbreaking. As a teenaged girl she'd killed her stepfather, an accident for which she had allowed her mother to take the rap and spend time behind bars. The lies had torn the family apart. Simone's grandfather hadn't spoken to her since then.

In comparison, Claire supposed her secret was not nearly so shocking. Still, it shamed her. A decade earlier she had met and married a man in a cowardly attempt to get out from underneath her father's thumb. The marriage hadn't lasted, nor had her spurt of rebellion. Both had been brief, their endings regrettable. She had only herself to blame for that.

Oh, she'd been genuinely fond of Ethan. At the time she had wondered if maybe she might be falling in love with the hard-working, sweet-talking young man who'd seemed so interested in her opinions, her dreams and her goals. No one before or since had taken her as seriously. God knew, she hadn't taken herself seriously, which made her treatment of Ethan all the more appalling.

She'd used him.

Worse than using him, she'd set him up—his David to her father's Goliath. Unlike the biblical version of the story, though, this time Goliath had come out the winner.

She hadn't seen or heard from Ethan since. Nor had she become deeply involved with anyone else, despite her father's efforts at finding her the perfect husband and her own attempts at dating. According to Belle, Claire was punishing herself. Simone had suggested she was waiting for a proper resolution to her marriage before moving on.

Closure. It was, they'd realized, what they all were seeking. And so, before their ride through China's Yunnan Province had ended, the three women had made a pact. They would make amends and then they would start over. Getting from point A to point B, however, would be no easy downhill ride. It would require an uphill trek over very rocky terrain.

For Claire, it meant taking full responsibility for her actions and for her life. She would face Ethan, return the ring that had been in her jewelry box all of these years and finally make the apology that had been owed to him for more than a decade. What would he say? she wondered. How would he react when she contacted him? Memories beckoned, at first sweet and then turning sour, just as their relationship had. She'd be kidding herself if she thought he was going to be happy to see her.

"Miss Mayfield," someone called. "Welcome home."

She glanced over to see Dolan, her father's driver, standing near the gate. Her gaze veered momentarily past his lanky, black-clad frame, but she recognized no one else. She chided herself for thinking her parents might have ventured to the airport to welcome her home. Sumner and Marianna Mayfield hadn't wanted her to go on the bike trek in the first place, regardless of its role in raising funds for charity.

Unseemly, her mother had called it. Just as she had found Claire's more sculpted physique unfeminine. Apparently it was better to be wisp thin and sickly all the time like herself.

During the months leading up to the trip, her father had appeared impressed by her dedication to the grueling training regimen she'd put together. Ultimately, though, he'd considered the entire endeavor unnecessary.

"Write a check, kitten," he'd suggested.

Checks took care of all sorts of things—even idealistic young men who were not deemed suitable hus-bands for the debutante daughter of a wealthy Chicago businessman.

Mayfields were good at writing checks. And Claire had been good at taking her parents' advice rather than risking her father's wrath or upsetting her mother, who was always suffering from some malady or another. This time, though, she'd held her ground. This time she'd been determined to do more than donate money, which God knew she had in abundance thanks to her trust fund. Instead, she'd decided to put herself to the test. She'd had something to prove—to the people who believed she would never have to earn her way, and to herself.

So far, she was happy with the results.

"I trust your trip was uneventful," Dolan inquired politely, taking the bag from her hands. The courtesy was second nature and one he was paid to perform. Even so, it startled Claire, who nearly snatched it back. In a matter of weeks, she had come to rely on herself.

"Not exactly."

She recalled the bruises, scrapes and blisters, many of which had not yet healed. Nothing about the trip had been easy, but even as she sighed, she was smiling. She hadn't felt this rejuvenated, this motivated, this damned purposeful in a very long time.

Dolan smiled in return, mistaking the meaning of her sigh. "Don't worry. I'll have you at your condo in short order. Traffic should be light this time of day. I'll have you sitting poolside, sipping an apple martini well before dinner."

Claire shook her head, though, and retrieved from her purse the folded classified section of the previous day's *Chicago Sun-Times*. She'd picked it up during her layover in Los Angeles and had already made the necessary calls to set up appointments with Realtors. Handing it to the driver, she said, "Actually, I need to make a couple of stops first."

Dolan's graying eyebrows rose as he studied the circled addresses. "Apartments, miss?" And she knew he was good and flummoxed when he overstepped his bounds by asking, "Why do you need to look at apartments?"

"I've decided to find a place in the city."

"In the city?" he repeated blankly.

Claire nodded. "I'm moving."

And this time that would involve more than having the staff tote her belongings to a condominium her parents owned not far from their sprawling suburban Chicago estate. She'd done that after the marriage fiasco. Looking back, she realized what a pitiful attempt at independence it had been. No wonder her parents hadn't tried to talk her out of it. This time they would.

Dolan's startled reaction was mild compared to what she suspected her parents' would be. Her father was going to erupt. After all, how could he continue to run her life if she was living an hour away in the city? Her mother would probably suffer one of her debilitating migraines brought on by emotional stress.

Claire wasn't looking forward to the coming confrontation any more than she was eager to contact Ethan. To hear his deep voice again. To lose herself in the vivid green of his eyes—eyes that no doubt would brim with condemnation.

"I can do it," she murmured.

"Pardon me, miss?"

She lifted her shoulders in a shrug. "Sometimes you just have to trust yourself, take your hand off the brake and let momentum carry you all the way down the hill."

She'd done that on the descent into Tiger Leaping Gorge, heart jammed in her throat and blocking her scream as the bike's narrow tires had raced over bumpy and winding cobblestone roads that hugged the mountain on one side and dropped away into the gorge on the other.

Safely at the bottom, she'd pumped her fists in the air and whooped in triumph. Of course, once the adrenaline rush had abated, she'd heaved the contents of her stomach on to the tops of her shoes.

Dolan eyed her curiously, but merely nodded. "Of course, miss."

He didn't have a clue what she was talking about. For that matter, Claire herself had only just begun to understand all of the lessons she'd learned.

She just hoped to God that when she found Ethan it would be far less painful and humiliating than when she'd hit that rock on the second day of their trip and wound up flying headfirst over the handlebars.

CHAPTER ONE

DID THE MAN have to be so good-looking?

That was Claire's first thought as she stared at the color photograph of Ethan Seaver.

It wasn't fair. He'd been approaching Greek god status a decade ago, with his deep-set green eyes, sexy mouth and well-defined cheekbones. He'd only improved with age.

The picture on the Web site was a head and shoulders shot, a professional portrait of a professional man. She could just make out the knot of a tie and the collar of a snowy-white shirt. She tried to concentrate on these innocuous details rather than the leanness of his cheeks or the sculpted line of his jaw. Even so, as she unscrewed the cap from a bottle of spring water and took a swig, she was wishing for something with a little more kick.

Locating her ex had proved remarkably simple. She hadn't even required the services of a private investigator. All she'd had to do was type Ethan's name into the search field on her laptop computer and hit Enter. Within seconds the search engine had spat back several screenfuls of possible matches to her rather broad inquiry.

The first couple of hits had provided links to newspaper stories, one from *The Detroit Free Press* and another from a respected national business journal. She had dismissed both at first, assuming it was a different Ethan Seaver who had been named as one of the thirty American entrepreneurs under forty to watch. But then her gaze had caught on the third entry down: Seaver Security Solutions, Ethan J. Seaver, president. Her heart had thumped and the blood had pounded noisily in her ears. Yet Claire swore she could hear his voice.

I plan to own my own company, Claire. A security firm protecting the assets of the Fortune 500. Some day even the likes of your father will be seeking my advice.

He'd told her that not long after proposing, as if wanting to assure her that his ambitions reached well beyond remaining a second-shift worker who punched a clock for somebody else.

According to the Web site, Ethan was the president and founder of a growing and respected commercial security firm that did everything from installation and monitoring to consulting and product development. Its headquarters was in Detroit with clients all over the Midwest.

Including Chicago.

Claire laughed out loud. The sound echoed off the bare walls of her apartment, a spacious two bedroom in a trendy section of Chicago that commanded a high price thanks to its sunrise view of Lake Michigan. Only a couple of days had passed since her return from the Himalayas, but she'd certainly managed to shake things up by signing a lease. As a result, her mother had taken to her bed and wasn't speaking to Claire. Unfortunately, her father was. He'd spent the better part of the morning trying to "talk some sense" into Claire as a crew of movers had carried her boxed-up belongings to a waiting van.

It had irritated Sumner to no end that this time, no matter how much he blustered or threatened, Claire hadn't budged. The problem—his problem, not hers—was that she'd never felt more sensible in her life.

Sensible. Yet here she was, sitting cross-legged on the bare floor and laughing like a happily medicated root canal patient because Ethan had essentially been right in her backyard all these years. Not only that, but he'd been providing surveillance and other high-end services to some of his ex-father-in-law's competitors. The payback quotient was subtle but there.

Of course, even a decade ago Ethan's dogged determination had been obvious. It was one of the qualities she had admired, respected. Claire had never met anyone quite like him in her sheltered life. He'd come from a modest background and yet words like "no" and "I can't" hadn't been part of his vocabulary. He'd been so driven, so purposeful. So…disappointing.

She rested the chilled bottle of water against her forehead, mirth and pride subsiding as anger sneaked in.

She had little doubt where Ethan had gotten the start-up capital for his business. She'd watched her father write out the postdated check. A very hefty sum paid to the order of Ethan Seaver on one condition: he needed to go away quickly and quietly.

And he had.

The one person Claire had counted on to be immune to her father's high-handed bullying, the one person she had assumed would be too proud to take the powerful Sumner Mayfield's money, had done just that, consenting to a divorce, keeping their marriage hush-hush, disappearing.

She swatted her anger aside. It didn't matter. These days, Claire was counting on herself. She should have done that back then too, instead of involving a third party in her sticky family dynamics.

Staring at Ethan's photograph, she swore his gaze held the same amount of accusation it had the last time they'd been face-to-face.

"Why in the hell did you marry me, Claire?" The demand had sounded almost like a challenge.

"I am sorry, Ethan," she murmured now to the image on the computer screen.

That doesn't count, honey.

Claire could almost hear Belle saying it, the words clipped with her British accent. She could almost hear Simone's laughter trill. How she missed them. She had other friends, of course, but none in whom she had confided her shameful secret. That made the bond they shared all the more special.

Then, as if she had conjured up the pair, her computer

chimed, signaling an e-mail had just been received. Claire clicked on her mailbox and discovered two, both delivered to the group account they had set up for their correspondence. The first message was from Simone and had come in several hours earlier. The latest was from Belle and apparently was in response to Simone's. The subject lines didn't bode well: *diary missing*.

Claire clicked on Simone's e-mail first:

Hullo, ladies. I'm embarrassed to admit this, but I seem to have lost the journal I kept during our trip.

Claire sucked in a breath. Simone had kept rather detailed notes of their travels, their burgeoning friendship and finally their secrets and what they planned to do about them. Now the diary was gone, apparently dropped at the airport in her rush to catch a taxi. It made Claire a little queasy to think someone might be reading it. She clicked open Belle's response:

Oh, Simone! What a shame about your diary. I know how hard you worked on it. Will you be able to put together your article without it?"

Simone worked for *Girl Talk* magazine.

If you need any details, I've got the stuff I wrote for my reports that you can have. As for anyone connecting us with it, I wouldn't worry too much. It's most likely in some airport waste compactor by now.

Probably, Claire thought. Even if someone had opened it, the beginning pages were likely bland enough to quell any interest.

Belle had continued,

Now for my news...

Claire blinked at the screen. And here she'd thought she had been working at a fast pace. But then, Belle never could stand to have anyone else in the lead. Already she'd left her husband, Ivo, moving out of his upscale Belgravia town house, and was living in the flat at Camden Lock she'd kept since before her marriage. And she'd cut her hair, changed her look. She'd attached a photograph that had Claire smiling. Belle's trademark blonde locks were gone, clipped off into a softly layered short 'do that complemented her lovely face.

Claire wrote back to Simone first:

Don't beat yourself up about this. It's disappointing and frustrating, but I can't imagine it will cause any problems for any of us.

She added a one-sided happy face. Then she wrote:

By the way, I moved out, too. I'm in my new apartment right now, sitting on the floor since I have no furniture yet. Not even a comfortable bed. Reminds me of our trip.

This time the smiley face icon was all teeth.

And, drum roll please. I've found my ex. Turns out he's made quite a name for himself. I'm attaching a URL to his Web site.

Send.

To her delight, Belle answered just as Claire was getting ready to log off. Apparently she was still online:

Hmm. A prime specimen, that one. I can see why you were attracted to him.

Claire ignored the tug of lust that lingered when she recalled his face…and remembered his very capable hands. She wrote back:

Wish me luck. I'm going to call him first thing tomorrow morning.

You're calling him? Why not a face-to-face meeting? He deserves that much, don't you think?

Belle's query nipped at Claire's conscience.

Yes, but I think I need to call first. He lives in another state now, a good six hours' drive.

A day's ride away. Take your bike.

Belle teased in return.

A little chilly for that here in November.

Freezing rain tapped at the windows as she typed the words.

Fine. Take a car then. But go.

Belle could be relentless.
Claire promised:

I will. Eventually. For now, a phone call.

Okay. For now. Let us know how it goes. It must be late in Chicago.

Nearly two in the morning.

Better get your beauty sleep then. Not that you need it. Good night, love.

'Night.

Claire jotted down Ethan's office number from the Web site and then turned off the computer. First thing in the morning, she vowed silently, she would speak to him.

* * *

Ethan Seaver believed in setting goals and going after what he wanted—even the seemingly impossible. That was how he explained his success in business when the odds had been stacked against him and his small independent company at the outset.

A man had to be determined, decisive. He had to be willing to take risks. He couldn't let the fear of failure hold him back. Ethan wasn't afraid to fail. In fact, he refused to accept it as an outcome. Professionally.

His personal life was another matter. He'd learned his lesson—a very painful one—a long time ago courtesy of a beautiful woman. Some risks just weren't worth taking, just as sometimes failure was the price one paid for being blind and foolish. His disastrous marriage to Claire Mayfield had taught him to be cautious—his sisters-in-law claimed suspicious—of women in general and love in particular. He dated, but he was careful to keep things from developing beyond a casual relationship. That suited him. After all, he didn't have time for more than dinners out and the occasional romantic evening in. Business was his main focus and his business was growing.

Seaver Security Solutions had posted record profits the previous year. Ethan wanted to expand the bottom line further by moving into new markets and beginning production of the new security system he'd developed. Record profits notwithstanding, he needed serious money to do that. He'd put out feelers, quietly seeking an investor, but he was having little luck finding one who shared his vision. Meanwhile, his accountant was suggesting he consider taking Seaver public.

"The initial public offering would bring in more than enough to cover your research and development needs," the accountant had assured him during a recent meeting. "It could even be a carrot to attract and retain quality workers if you compensated your top managers and executives with stock as well as a competitive salary."

It made sense. Still, Ethan wasn't entirely comfortable with the idea of sharing the fruits of his labor with outsiders. Nor was he sure he wanted the added headache of filing regular reports with the Securities and Exchange Commission, even though a publicly held Seaver Security Solutions would certainly enjoy greater prestige.

He was flipping through the prospectus he'd had a team of lawyers draft just in case when his secretary buzzed him on the office intercom.

"There's a call for you, Mr Seaver."

He glanced at his watch. Not quite seven-thirty. He liked to start his work day early, by seven at the latest. He found himself most productive before ten. Curiously, he'd met few movers and shakers in the business world his security firm served who believed likewise, unless it involved a meeting on a golf course.

"Who is it?" he asked.

"Claire Mayfield."

Ethan prided himself on having nerves of steel and a poker face. He routinely cleaned up in Friday night card games with his two brothers and their friends. But nothing could have prepared him for hearing that name. It blasted from his past, landing like a sucker punch. He was grateful to be alone in his office since his mouth had slackened with surprise. He snapped it shut and tamped down on the unexpected and unwanted flood of emotions.

He pressed the intercom button again. "Claire Mayfield?" he managed in a casual tone.

"She claims you know her," Anita Dauber replied.

Hardly, he thought. Bitterness welled again, spew-ing with the destructive force of molten lava. *I never knew the woman at all.* He cleared his throat. He was calm once again when he inquired, "Does she say why she's calling?"

"Just that it's personal. Should I ask her to be more specific?"

God, no! The last thing he wanted was to have his private life paraded in front of an employee, no matter how discreet Anita could be. He'd only told his immediate family about his hasty nuptials to Claire, and even then he'd skimped on the particulars. The outcome had been too embarrassing, too—painful, to give a detailed account.

"That's all right. I'll speak to her."

Ethan let Claire stew on hold for a good five minutes, almost hoping the uninspired instrumental versions of pop tunes piped through the line would get to her and she would hang up. But the light on his phone contin-ued to blink. It was just his luck. For once, the woman wasn't going away.

Let's get this over with.

He snatched up the receiver. "What can I do for you, Claire?"

Not bad, he decided. He came across as busy, impatient, maybe even a little bit bored. She, on the other hand, sounded just as he remembered when she said his name: sexy as hell with that smoky, throaty tone.

"Ethan. How are you?"

He leaned back in his chair, resting one ankle across the opposite knee, and ignored the tug of lust. "Fine, but a little surprised. I have to tell you, Claire, I didn't figure you'd even remember me after all this time."

"I remember you."

Because her tone had gone soft, he hardened his. "I remember you, too." Not fondly was implied. "So, to what do I owe the...pleasure?"

"I need to speak with you."

"Mayfield in the market for a new security system? Hope you're not counting on the family discount."

She ignored the insult, which made him feel small for issuing it in the first place. "No. Actually, it's a... personal matter."

He planted both feet on the floor again and straightened. "Nothing between us was *ever* personal."

"We were married," she said.

"Do a couple of days spent as husband and wife qualify as a real marriage?" he asked softly.

"It felt like the real thing at the time."

The words surprised him. They sneaked past his

defenses and made him remember things best left forgotten.

"Well, you'd have more experience in that regard than me," he replied.

"What do you mean by that?"

She sounded honestly baffled. He had no intention of enlightening her since it would involve delving into their past. "Look, Claire, I'm busy."

"I know. I checked out your company's Web site, by the way." There was a smile in her voice when she added, "Seaver Security Solutions is quite a success. You must be very proud."

"I am." After a brief pause, he said, "Is that what you called to tell me?"

"No. Actually, I...I have something of yours I need to return and some things I'd like to say. I'm calling to set up a meeting, perhaps later this week. I promise not to take up much of your time."

"You already have," he informed her. "Besides, I'll be out of the office later this week."

"Next week, then."

"Next week too. Whatever you have of mine I haven't missed it, so there's no need to return it. As for what you want to tell me after all these years, I'm listening."

"It's hard to explain, especially over the telephone."

His curiosity was well and truly stoked but he replied blandly, "Try, because this is the only opportunity I'm going to give you."

On the other end of the line, Claire paced in front of the large window in her apartment's living room. Outside, the sun was just coming up, spreading a warm amber glow over the velvety smooth waters of Lake Michigan. Inside, her emotions were choppy and churning. This wasn't going as she had hoped. She'd rehearsed what she'd planned to say, knew the words by heart. The problem was that Ethan was refusing to go along with her script and she was just no good at ad-libbing.

"Well?" he prompted as she continued to grope for the right words.

Claire studied the simple gold band she held between her index finger and thumb. "I…I regret the way things turned out between us. I never meant to hurt you."

"You didn't hurt me." Ethan's harsh laughter scraped against her ear. "Hell, you get right down to it, Claire, we hardly knew one another."

Hardly knew one another? There were times when she'd thought he could see into her soul. In a few short weeks, she'd sworn he'd understood her better than anyone else ever had.

"You ticked me off, sure," he continued conversationally. "I have wondered, though."

She swallowed. "About what?"

"Why me? What made you pick me? I mean, there had to have been other guys who were, shall we say, more in your league?" He made a humming noise. "Hell, maybe that was my appeal. Blue-collar background, dirt under the nails so to speak, a little rough around the edges socially. I suppose I provided what you would call shock value."

"No." Though he couldn't see her, Claire shook her head vehemently. "I…I liked you, Ethan. Really. I liked you a lot."

He snorted. "You *liked* me. I hope you haven't made it a habit to marry every man you like." His voice lowered. "But then you didn't marry me because you liked me, did you, Claire?"

"No." One small word, and yet she all but choked on it.

"You used me."

She squeezed her eyes shut, ashamed. He'd known. Of course he'd known. "I'm sorry, Ethan. Truly, I am. I acted badly, selfishly. I put you in a very awkward position because I was immature."

In response to her heartfelt mea culpa, all he offered was a bland, "Yes."

She tamped down the beginnings of temper. It wasn't as if Ethan hadn't gotten something for his trouble. She remembered the check. He'd had it in his hand, hadn't even tried to hide it as he'd let her walk away.

Claire studied the gold band in her own hand. This was about *her* behavior, not his.

"I am sorry," she managed again.

"Why?"

Claire frowned. "I think I just explained why."

"I guess I mean, why apologize now? It's been, what, ten years? Excuse me for suspecting an ulterior motive here, but it seems strange that, after all this time, you are suddenly calling me to say you're sorry."

Claire caught her reflection in the window's glass. A woman with short, sassy hair and an angled-up chin that bespoke confidence stared back.

"I've changed."

He was quiet for a long moment. "Me, too, Claire. I've changed, too. Don't contact me again. Unless, of course, it's to discuss business. In that case, I'll be more than happy to give your father a quote for a new security system, either for Mayfield's Chicago headquarters or any of its other sites in the United States or abroad."

"It wouldn't bother you to take his money?" she asked quietly, though she already knew the answer.

"Not in the least. Goodbye."

"Ethan—"

But he'd already hung up. The dial tone had switched to an agitated beep before Claire finally placed the cordless receiver back on its charger.

Disappointed, that was how she felt. She'd expected to experience a vastly different emotion once she'd contacted him, confronted her past. Instead of moving forward, though, she was stuck in Neutral.

"I said I was sorry," she murmured. It dawned on her that he'd never accepted her apology. "But he would accept a check."

She prowled her apartment, too restless to sit still. Not that she had much of anything to sit on. She had no furniture, although she had picked out a couch, chairs and an ottoman for the living room, as well as a cherry bedroom suite. It would be several weeks yet before any of it would be delivered. The bare walls and floors didn't lend any hominess to the place. Indeed, they added to her sense of isolation. She paced to the bedroom, where a queen-sized mattress and box spring were pushed against one wall. At least she wasn't sleeping on the floor any longer.

But she was sleeping alone.

For the first time in years she allowed herself to recall the way it had felt to slumber next to Ethan and to wake with his heavy arm draped across her torso. The gesture had seemed protective rather than possessive, just as the caresses had been patient and instructive as well as seductive.

She shivered now. She'd trembled then.

I promise I'll make you happy, Claire.

Caught up in the moment, caught up in the magic, she'd promised him the same. Another vow that both of them had broken.

Angry with Ethan, but more angry with herself, Claire tossed her workout clothes into a duffel bag and tugged a baseball cap low over her brow, leaving her short locks to sprout out the sides. She didn't bother with makeup. She left for the gym she belonged to across town, determined to exorcise old demons and sweat away her frustration and self-directed irritation on a stationary bike.

An hour later, as she pedaled furiously, perspiration

slicking her brow and sliding down her spine to soak the waist of her cotton workout shorts, Claire didn't miss the irony that, just as with her ex-husband, she was getting absolutely nowhere.

Ethan thought he had come so far since his short-lived and foolishly impulsive marriage to Claire, but merely hearing her voice that morning had yanked him backward and left him dangling from the same high precipice he'd fallen off a decade earlier.

It had been nearly two hours since her telephone call and he still couldn't get his mind to settle or his memory to shut off. Recollections from their past haunted him. Snippets from their conversation nagged.

"I'm sorry."

He had to admit, the apology had come as a complete surprise. Even more shocking, though, had been the fact that Claire hadn't denied using him. Nor had she tried to foist the blame for the fiasco that had been their marriage onto anyone else. No. She'd accepted full responsibility for behavior she'd readily conceded was selfish and immature.

Why didn't that make him feel any better? Why was he still sitting at his desk two hours later poking at her every word with the same morbid fascination of a gawker slowing down at the site of a car wreck?

Why hadn't he just said, *Apology accepted, nice knowing you,* and let it go at that?

Perhaps because she'd also claimed, *"I've changed."*

The words had him wondering. They had him curious.

Changed? What exactly did she mean by that? Had she grown a conscience? Or had she, too, at odd times over the past decade, found herself wondering where he was, what he was doing, if he was happy?

She'd been the only woman who'd ever made him fall so hard and fast. Love at first sight? Not exactly, but damned close. Ethan shoved a hand through his hair in disgust and sipped his coffee. The usually mild blend seemed as bitter as his mood. Well, whatever the reason for her call, he wasn't about to find himself in the same room as Claire Mayfield again.

It wasn't like him to avoid confrontation. Claire, of course, had a way of making him do things that were out of character. Like marrying her after only a handful of dates. Like seeking a divorce mere days after making what he'd thought would be a lifetime commitment.

I, Ethan James Seaver, take thee, Claire Anne Mayfield, as my lawfully wedded wife…

Even though he didn't want to remember, he was tugged back in time. He'd been twenty-six, determined to take on the world even though he'd been a mere security guard working second shift at the Mayfield corporate headquarters in Chicago. The family-owned company manufactured everything from toothpaste to pharmaceuticals with operations in seventeen countries around the globe. Claire had been twenty-one, reserved to the point of shyness. She'd been vulnerable, delicate, the kind of woman a man felt he needed to protect.

And she'd been beautiful.

Her hair had hung nearly to her waist, a dark veil of sorts behind which she'd seemed to hide. Once they'd properly met it had been his habit to push it away from her face and tuck it behind her ears so that he could see her better. The first time he'd done it, her eyes had grown wide. Then she'd smiled slowly and he'd felt the earth shift under his feet. She was the only woman who'd ever had that effect on him. He told himself he didn't miss that feeling of being out of control, that feeling of being...lost.

Claire had been doing an internship in the marketing department at Mayfield that summer. Each day, she'd left work at precisely five-thirty—the same time that Ethan took his dinner break in the employees' cafeteria. She'd always stopped in for a bottle of water to drink on the drive home. At first, Ethan hadn't known who Claire was, not that her identity would have mattered much or ended the attraction. He might have grown up poor on Chicago's south side, but even back then he'd had no shortage of confidence, no dearth of pride.

He'd never considered that he might not be "good enough" for her. What did it matter that his diploma had come from a community college rather than the Ivy League? What did it matter that her family's name regularly appeared in the newspaper, announcing Mayfield's many innovations and triumphs, whereas the only time the Seaver name had made the *Sun-Times* or *Tribune* it had been in the obituaries?

Everett Daniel Seaver, beloved husband of Mary, doting father of Ethan, Michael and James, died on Monday as the result of a motorcycle accident. In lieu of flowers, the family requests donations be made to the family to cover funeral expenses.

Ethan had been in elementary school and, at eleven, the oldest. His father had held a low-paying job. He'd had no life insurance, no savings put away. He'd left behind a heap of credit-card debt and a devastated wife who had barely managed to keep their family intact. In fact, for a little while Mary Seaver had been so broken that she hadn't managed at all. Ethan still remembered the confusion, the fear he and his brothers had experienced when the authorities had come to take them to foster care.

He'd been determined not to repeat his father's mistakes. He'd planned to make something of himself. In fact, he'd considered himself well on his way with a college degree under his belt and a growing bank account with which he planned to start his own business. So, after a week of his polite nods and her sidelong glances, he'd asked Claire for her telephone number. She'd blushed as she'd written it out on a paper napkin for him.

Their first date, if it could be called a date since it had occurred during his forty-five-minute dinner break, had ended with a polite handshake while she'd waited for her father's driver to arrive at Mayfield's front entrance. He could still recall the way her slim fingers had brushed against his rough palm as she'd pulled away. He'd never been so turned on in all his life.

The second date had ended with a brief kiss that nonetheless had heated his blood from simmering to a rolling boil and had made him desperate for much, much more. Barely a month afterward he'd asked her to marry him. It wasn't until later that he'd realized Claire actually had been the one to bring up the subject of matrimony.

Memories he'd long kept buried resurrected themselves now. He recalled the way she'd looked during their hasty Las Vegas wedding—small, delicate, her dark hair twisted into a clever knot at the back of her head that kept it away from her face. Her gold-flecked brown eyes had been luminous.

She hadn't worn the traditional bridal gown, but a simple suit whose pencil skirt tapered to the knee. It had been white, a fitting color he'd discovered later when they'd been alone in their hotel room, consummating the vows they'd just spoken. For a brief time, he'd counted himself the luckiest man in the world and he'd looked forward to building a future together.

…Till death us do part.

The words rang in Ethan's head and snapped him back to the present. He scrubbed a hand over his face. A fool, that was what he'd been. Played from beginning to end by someone who might have been innocent but had been no novice at getting what she'd wanted.

He'd let himself be taken in by her slow smile and wide eyes. But Claire hadn't loved him. She hadn't planned to stay married to him, he'd learned soon enough. Ethan had been a means to an end, a payback, according to her father, who had arrived at their hotel suite late the following day.

Sumner Mayfield had come to take her home. He'd pulled her aside. Words had been spoken. Ethan had thought he heard Claire's mother mentioned. Then Claire had turned, smiled sadly.

"I have to go."

"Don't leave, Claire." Something had told Ethan that if she went now, she wouldn't be back.

"Think about your mother," her father said. Ethan watched her swallow and stifle a sob. Then she fled to the bedroom where the sheets were still warm from their lovemaking.

In the sitting area Sumner Mayfield explained his daughter's "rash" behavior to a thunderstruck Ethan.

"I'm afraid she's not happy with her fiancé right now."

"Fiancé?" The word had all but choked Ethan when he uttered it. No. The man was mistaken. He had to be. "She's not engaged."

"I'm sorry, son," Sumner said. "His name is Ashton Beaumont. They've known each other for years. Our families have always been close."

"Ashton Beaumont," he mumbled.

"Yes. Perhaps you've heard of his father. Rolland Beaumont owns a few dozen television and radio stations around the country. Ashton is being primed to take over after his father's retirement in a few years."

"I've heard of the Beaumonts." And, while Ethan

had always considered himself any man's equal, he knew a paralyzing moment of self-doubt and insecurity. Later, as much as for her lies, he'd resented Claire for that. "So, when were they supposed to marry?"

"Well, that's the problem. Ashton wants to wait till she graduates from college in a couple of years. Sensible man." Sumner nodded thoughtfully. "You know, she needs to grow up a little more and enjoy some independence before settling down."

"She seems ready enough," he countered. But the statement had been made with more bravado than confidence.

"Yes, she thinks so," Sumner agreed. He sighed wearily. "Her heart's been set on being a June bride. *This* June. It looks like she got her wish."

"That's right. She's *my* wife now." Ethan crossed his arms, braced his legs. The last stand of a doomed man.

"I know." Sumner nodded. "But for how long, son? Do you really think she plans to stay married to you? Your backgrounds, your lifestyles, they're simply incompatible."

Ethan's arms dropped to his sides, although his hands remained fisted.

"Claire can be surprisingly impulsive," Sumner continued. "She's regretting this hasty marriage already, believe me. She wanted to make Ashton see reason. She never intended for things to get this far."

Ethan said nothing. Instead, he fingered the simple and inexpensive band of gold on his left hand. Claire was wearing its twin.

"I know my daughter." Sumner's tone and his expression were appallingly sympathetic as he stepped for-ward to rest one hand on Ethan's shoulder. "That's why I'm here."

While Ethan stood there—stupefied and numb—Sumner wrote out a check.

"For your trouble," he said, tucking it into Ethan's hand.

When he turned, Claire was standing in the bedroom doorway. Her hair was loose, partially obscuring her face. Still, he saw the truth clearly enough in the flush of color that stained her cheeks.

Words were exchanged, although exactly what had been said, he could no longer remember. Only that he had ached after he'd watched her follow her father out the door.

They hadn't spoken again, although when he'd returned to Chicago he'd had a visit from her family's attorney. Ethan's employment with the company that provided security for Mayfield was terminated—dereliction of duty cited as the reason. He could have protested it, but why bother? Just as he could have objected when he'd been asked to sign divorce papers. He hadn't. In short order Claire Seaver had become Claire Mayfield once again. Ethan had moved to Detroit, where he'd worked like a dog to start his own business.

He'd been trying his damnedest to forget the woman ever since, and he'd been doing a fair job of it…until today.

CHAPTER TWO

SUMNER MAYFIELD WAS average height and a little on the heavy side. He carried his weight well, though, thanks to broad shoulders and cleverly tailored clothes that helped hide his widening girth. To Claire, her father had always been larger than life, someone she had feared as much as she had revered. Today, as she sat across from him in his office in the Mayfield headquarters building, she noted the deep lines that fanned from his eyes and the thinning hair. He'd grown older, she realized. And she'd finally grown up.

"Your mother was wondering if you'd be by for dinner this evening," he said.

"I have plans." She didn't, but neither did she intend to subject herself to an evening of badgering and emotional blackmail. "Sorry."

"You disappoint me, Claire. Aren't you even going to ask how she is?"

"Has she recovered from her migraine?"

"Thankfully, yes. She's been in bed for days, you

know. Even the prescription the doctor gave her failed to take the edge off for more than a day." His tone held accusation.

"Why is that my fault, Dad?" He always did this, both of her parents did. They tried to make her feel guilty and responsible, as if her mother's very survival depended on Claire toeing the line.

"Well, your current behavior certainly isn't helping matters. You know how delicate her health is."

Claire sucked in a breath, held it a moment before exhaling slowly through her teeth.

"I'm not here to talk about Mother. I'm here to discuss business. I want you to reconsider my application for vice president of new product development for our North American market."

"Kitten, we've been over this," he said condescendingly. "Before you left for the Himalayas I explained why I passed you over. You're just not ready."

"Clive thinks I am," she said, invoking the name of the department's executive head. He was set to retire by the end of the year, at which time the current vice president would take his place, creating the opening Claire sought. Clive said she reminded him a lot of her father.

"You have great instincts," he'd told her a couple of months back when he'd encouraged her to approach her father.

Sumner didn't share his opinion.

"I think you need more time," he said, steepling his

fingers. "Besides, Roger Fleming has been in the department longer."

"So longevity trumps ingenuity? For goodness' sake, Dad, Roger Fleming wouldn't recognize innovation if it bit him in the butt," she countered. Claire had ideas. She saw potential for greater opportunities for Mayfield to move into so-called green products that were more environmentally friendly. It was a largely untapped market for the company. "Mayfield is on the cusp. We can embrace change or we can watch our customer base continue to erode."

"Some of our products face stiff competition," Sumner conceded. "But overall we're solid."

"Dinosaurs were solid too. Look what happened to them."

He snorted. "Mayfield is never going to become extinct."

"Maybe not extinct, but we're following where we used to be leading. You've told me often enough that Granddad was a pioneer. That spirit has been lost. We're reacting to our competitors, rather than being proactive and forcing them to react to us. I can be a great asset to this company if given half a chance."

After that impassioned monologue, Sumner merely shook his head. "I'm sorry, Claire. My mind is made up. Maybe in another couple of years you'll be ready for a position like that. For now, I think you need more…seasoning."

"Another couple of years?" She thought about the

bike trip, the hours she'd cycled, the distance she'd traveled in more ways than could be measured in miles or kilometers. She couldn't tolerate the status quo any longer. "I'm sorry too, Dad, because you leave me no choice but to look for work elsewhere."

Sumner looked amused by her bold declaration. "And where would you go, kitten?"

She gritted her teeth at the childish nickname. Even now he didn't see her as an adult. "I'm not sure, but I don't think I'll have a problem getting a job."

"Oh, really?"

"As you've always told me, Dad, the Mayfield name opens doors."

Sumner glowered in response. "Don't threaten me, young lady," he admonished, standing so he could lean forward to rest his hands on the desk.

It was a tactic she'd seen him use often in the board-room, generally with favorable results. It didn't work on Claire—this time. She rose to her feet as well.

"I'm not threatening you." She kept her voice calm, her gaze steady lest he accuse her of being hysterical. Her father could be disgustingly sexist, a character trait Claire's mother enabled with her feebleness. "I'm stating fact. I want to stay at Mayfield. That goes without saying. But only if you finally start taking me seriously and recognize that I have real contributions to make."

"Perhaps I'd take you more seriously if you'd settle down and stop acting so outrageously. Moving into the city, breaking your mother's heart."

"What's outrageous about wanting to run my own life? I could be the best thing to happen to product development in a long time if you'd stop treating me like I'm twelve and start remembering that I have a master's degree in business. As a Mayfield, I have a stake in this company, which is why I've stayed even after watching less qualified people be promoted above me. I want a position that reflects my capabilities and challenges my potential. If I can't get that at Mayfield, then I'll go elsewhere to meet my needs."

"Your *needs?*" He levered himself away from the desk and walked to the window. Over one shoulder he asked, "What do you need, Claire? Your mother and I have given you everything you could ever want."

"Except the freedom to push myself," she said quietly. "That's what I liked about the Himalayas trip. For the first time in my life, being a Mayfield wasn't enough. I had no one else to fall back on." She thought of Ethan when she added, "I had no one to use." And then she thought of her parents. "I had no one to blame. It all came down to me, to my stamina, to my skills and to my sheer will."

"It was just a bike ride."

She shook her head. He still didn't get it. "You know, Dad, I've never considered myself to be very much like you. Everyone has always told me I'm the picture of Mother, soft-spoken and delicately built. For a while, I started to believe that I needed to be cared for, looked after. But you know what? I inherited some of your steel after all. I'll give you until the end of the week to reconsider the promotion. I won't take no for an answer this time."

He issued an oath. "I don't know what's gotten into you."

Her smile was sad. "I know you don't, but I do."

Early the next morning, Claire sat alone at a table in Café Connections, an Internet coffeehouse within walking distance of her apartment. Her life certainly was in chaos, which she recognized and accepted as a necessary first step to true change. Recognizing and accepting, of course, weren't the same as liking. She'd spent a sleepless night trying to figure out how to tidy up the current mess so she could move on. She sipped a cup of French roast and considered her options.

"I won't take no for an answer."

She'd told her father that yesterday. Maybe she should have said the same thing to Ethan when they'd spoken earlier in the week. Despite offering an apology, nothing between them felt remotely resolved. In fact, quite the opposite.

She needed encouragement. She needed advice. And so she booted up her laptop, logged on to the Internet and wrote an e-mail to Simone and Belle.

Lots to report in the past week here...

She summarized the meeting with her father and then the conversation with Ethan.

We spoke on the telephone—and before you say anything, Belle, he refused to meet with me, so he left me little choice but to do my groveling over the phone. I said I was sorry. He didn't appear moved by the apology. The exchange was relatively brief.

She sipped her coffee, recalling that there had been a time when they'd been able to talk for hours.

And not all that polite.

Just as there was a time when he'd been solicitous, gentlemanly.

Claire glanced out of the window for a moment, watching the traffic speed by and the pedestrians file past. They all seemed to know where they were going.

I don't feel any better, she confided. I don't feel like I've resolved anything. In fact, I realized as I spoke with Ethan that I'm still a little bitter that he took that damned check from my father.

And she was.

She remembered seeing it in his hand, a pale green slip of paper that had sealed their fate. Ethan hadn't refused it or torn it to bits as she'd expected him to, had wanted him to. The dollar amount had been visible, and though it was a princely sum, her only thought had been: *is that all I'm worth?*

"Things are easily taken care of in your world, aren't they?" he had the nerve to say, sounding angry.

She shook her head. "No."

"Are you going to stand there and tell me you planned to stay married to me?"

The truth was she hadn't been sure…not until the previous night when he'd made love to her with such tender conviction. Her face heated and she was too embarrassed, felt too exposed to share that thought with him. He apparently took her flaming cheeks to mean something else.

"Claire." Her father was at the door to their hotel suite, holding it open, impatient to be on his way. "We need to leave. Now. You're Mother is waiting."

"Better go, kitten." Ethan's lips twisted as he used her father's nickname for her. He knew, of course, how much she despised it. "No need to keep slumming now that you've made your point."

Claire didn't understand what he'd meant by that nasty comment, but her father ushered her out before she could ask. On the flight home, she was so confused. What did she want to happen now? What exactly had she expected to happen between her and Ethan after their hasty nuptials? She hadn't thought that far ahead.

Later, when it had become clear she would never see Ethan again, she'd felt disappointed, disillusioned. Finally, all that had remained was shame and regret for her behavior. Apparently anger had been hiding in there as well.

She wrote:

So, what do you guys think? Do I try again? And, if so, how do you suggest I go about it?

Send.

She sipped her coffee and waited for a response. Belle would be done for the day at the television studio, her London morning talk show long off air. As for Simone, she'd probably be kicking back in her Melbourne apartment after a long day at work at the magazine.

Belle's message came through as Claire finished a second cup of coffee.

Do I try again?!

Belle typed the words in bold letters and Claire pictured the other woman putting her hands on her hips.

What kind of question is that? If you don't feel you've reached a resolution, of course you try again. Show up at the man's door if necessary. Have your say. You'll never find peace otherwise. Trust me on this, Claire.

Belle was right. She checked her watch. She needed to get to work. She was preparing to log off when Simone's e-mail popped into her in-box.

Urgent!

The subject line had adrenaline shooting through

Claire's system and that was before she'd read the e-mail's contents.

"Oh, no!" The words slipped out on a moan.

Just when Claire thought her life couldn't get more disordered and chaotic, it turned out Simone's journal had not made its way, unread, into an airport Dumpster as they'd all hoped. It had been found, opened, its contents possibly perused. The book into which her friend had meticulously documented their physical journey as well as their deepest, darkest secrets had turned up in the hands of a stranger who was now privy to their most intimate thoughts. Not just any stranger, either. A journalist named Ryan Tanner.

Poor Simone. She was convinced that Ryan had read her every word—and that he would print the story.

Claire shuddered then as a thought occurred to her. Australia was half a world away, but Claire's father's business was international. Mayfield had subsidiaries around the globe, including a manufacturing plant in Melbourne. And then there was Ethan. He was a small fish compared to her father, but his security firm was beginning to take off in the States. One of the thirty under forty to watch, she recalled from the news article she'd read online.

What if…?

Claire rubbed the center of her forehead, where the beginnings of a headache throbbed in time with her speeding heart. What if some enterprising journalist here managed to get wind of the story? She wasn't being dramatic or paranoid. Internet search engines turned up all sorts of things. Wasn't that how she'd found Ethan in the first place?

She would need to let them know. Both of them.

She had little doubt that her father was going to be furious, but it wasn't his reaction to the news that concerned Claire. He had a team of lawyers to threaten lawsuits and, if that failed, a public relations department that would do its damnedest to spin whatever articles came out into a positive light. Ethan, however, was another matter. What if Ethan couldn't mount the same offensive should the American media pick up on the story?

He could be ruined. A business such as his, after all, was built on personal integrity and trust. Would clients trust the instincts and advice of a man who'd once let himself be duped into marriage? Wouldn't they question the integrity of a man who had taken a check to get a quickie divorce and then parlayed his payoff into a business?

Claire's headache became full-blown. All she had wanted to do was right a past wrong. That was all Belle and Simone wanted to do as well. No good deed, she thought. She recalled her earlier conversation with Ethan. His suspicions, his accusations.

Was it a good deed? Maybe it was just another form of selfishness. After all, it was *her* need to unburden *her* conscience that could wind up destroying Ethan or at least costing him dearly. The forgiveness Claire had been seeking seemed a long shot now, but it was no longer her primary motivation.

Ethan didn't want to see her and he'd made it clear he wasn't interested in accepting an apology for what she'd done. But he needed to know that the past he apparently wanted to forget could wind up public knowledge.

Claire packed up her computer and hurried back to her apartment.

"Out of town?" Vaguely she recalled Ethan saying something about going away, but she'd assumed it was an excuse for not agreeing to a meeting. "For how long?" she asked his secretary now.

"Until after Thanksgiving."

"But that's more than two weeks away." This matter couldn't wait that long. "Do you have a number where I can reach him?"

"Sorry, he's at his vacation home and I can't give out that information. I can relay a message if it's something that requires his immediate attention," the woman offered.

It was and it did, but Claire wasn't about to let someone else deliver this news. She hung up the telephone, but she didn't give up. His secretary's mention of his vacation home had sparked Claire's memory. She did another search on the computer, scrolling down until she found the entry she was seeking. It was a feature article that had appeared in a men's magazine. In it Ethan had mentioned spending time in Glen Arbor, a trendy, upscale vacation community about five hours north of Detroit.

"Gotcha!" she said, simultaneously relieved and distressed, because this time, she decided, she would face him in person.

A few clicks of the computer later and Claire had booked a flight from Chicago to a small airport just north of Glen Arbor and arranged for a rental car. Her plane would depart from Midway that evening.

Claire wasn't sure what to pack or how long she would be gone. Most likely she would be back in Chicago by the next afternoon, her mission accomplished. Even so, she filled one suitcase with several changes of clothes. What did one wear for an occasion such as this? Just before leaving, she pulled the simple gold band from the bottom drawer in her jewelry box.

I, Ethan James Seaver, take thee, Claire Anne Mayfield...

Even as she slipped it on her finger, she knew the time had come to return it.

Claire stopped at Mayfield on the way to the airport.

"Keep the meter running," she told the cab driver.

She didn't know how long the meeting with her father would last, but she wanted to be able to leave quickly once she'd delivered the bad news. She saw no need to stick around for the inevitable long-winded diatribe. It was just her luck that he launched into one almost immediately.

"Good heavens, kitten!" Sumner thundered. His ruddy face turned the color of a ripe eggplant. "What were you thinking? Why would you even bring up that matter? It's ancient history, and something I went to a great deal of trouble to take care of, I might add."

Yes, she thought ruefully. He'd spared no expense.

"It's not ancient history to me. It's bothered me for a long time now, Dad." She hoped that for once he might actually listen to what she had to say. She hoped that for once he might actually understand. She took a deep breath, deciding to confess all. "In fact, I called—"

Sumner steamrolled over her explanation in his typical overbearing style and invoked Marianna's fragile health for good measure. "I don't know what this is going to do to your mother. She's only just started feeling well. You barely know those women, for goodness' sake. What possessed you to confide that stupid bit of teenaged rebellion?"

"I wasn't a teenager." She'd been old enough to know better.

"You might as well have been."

She sucked in a breath. "Well, Belle and Simone are my friends. Friends tell each other things. That's how it works, you know?" And yet she'd never told any of her other friends about Ethan.

"Friends," Sumner sneered. "They barely rate as acquaintances. You pedaled a bike alongside them for—what?—a couple of weeks."

He made it sound as if the three women had taken a leisurely afternoon ride through a park. As for the relatively short length of time she'd known them, it didn't matter to Claire. Their bond was solidly rooted. Sometimes people met and they just clicked. It had happened that fast with Simone and Belle.

Claire swallowed hard as a question whispered from her subconscious: Had that been the case with Ethan? Had they just clicked?

Her father's tirade continued. "For all you know, this Simone woman could have planned something like this from the beginning. You are a Mayfield, after all. Even halfway around the world our name means something. People hear it and they see dollar signs."

"Look, Dad!" she shouted, rising to her feet. "I can assure you this wasn't intentional. Belle and Simone have a lot to lose should the secrets in that journal get out. This wasn't some kind of setup."

"Just a costly foul-up, then," he finished. Bristly gray brows arched and he stood up so that he could peer down his nose at her. "Do you still think you should be second in command of one of Mayfield's most important divisions?"

"One has nothing to do with the other."

He only shook his head dismissively. "I think for the time being you can assume that the issue of a promotion has been taken off the table."

"As if it was ever on."

"I might have considered it."

She wanted to believe him. "I told you I would leave Mayfield and look for a job elsewhere. I meant it."

Claire's pride might have been in tatters, her life might have been falling to pieces, but after she reminded him of her ultimatum she crossed her arms and met his gaze squarely.

Sumner merely smiled. "Business is a lot like poker, kitten. Never bet what you're not willing to lose."

He chucked her chin then and settled back in his seat, apparently thinking he'd called her bluff.

Later that day, as Claire waited for her bags to come around on the luggage carousel in the airport in Traverse City, Michigan, she decided it had almost been worth becoming unemployed to see the look on her father's face when she'd tendered her resignation, effective immediately.

CHAPTER THREE

ETHAN STOOD ON the deck of his home just east of Glen Arbor. There were larger homes in the area, multimillion dollar ones perched on the shores of Big and Little Glen and dotting the Lake Michigan coast just over the huge dunes to the west. But, as far as he was concerned, none had a better view than his.

He'd purchased the wooded acreage on the high ridge just after the real estate market had begun to take off in the area. It had cost what he'd considered a king's ransom back then. Now its value had more than tripled and that was before he'd had his spacious house built.

The four-bedroom two-story was an authentic log home. Some of the red pines used in the construction measured nearly three feet in diameter and had been cut from forests in the Upper Peninsula. The bark had been stripped away by patient, skilled hands to reveal honey-colored logs that had then been scored one to the other so that they fit snugly and required no mortar or nails. Solid, that was what it was. That was why he liked it.

The home's top floor was divided into two wings that kept the master suite private from the guest quarters. One of those rooms soon would be occupied. His youngest brother and sister-in-law were due to arrive in another day for a couple of days of rest and relaxation. Ethan didn't figure his quiet mornings would be interrupted much. James and Laura were technically still newlyweds, married just over a year, with a baby due at Christmas. They tended to sleep late and keep to themselves.

It would be a different story if his brother Michael, sister-in-law Melissa and their brood of three preschool-age tots were on hand. Peace and quiet would be a scarce commodity then. Not like this morning when the only sounds to breach the silence were the distant squawk of blue jays and the rustle of squirrels as they foraged for acorns beneath the blanket of leaves on the forest floor.

A storm was forecast for later in the morning, but at the moment the post-dawn air was crisp and still. From his high vantage point Ethan could see the choppy surfaces of Big and Little Glen Lakes. Farther out on the horizon, fat thunderclouds the color of overripe plums were rolling in from Lake Michigan. They fit his mood.

He hadn't been able to stop thinking about Claire, no matter how hard he'd tried. The woman was like a splinter, under his skin and bothering him. He kept hearing that smoky voice, picturing the long curtain of her hair, remembering the soft satin of her pale skin.

"I need to get out more," he muttered aloud.

He'd dreamed about her last night. It wasn't the first dream in which she'd featured over the years, but it had been one of the most erotic. He'd woken up aroused and frustrated, angry with her, angry with himself. Worst of all, though, he'd felt lonely, as if something were missing from his life. He didn't like that. He had everything he wanted, everything he needed.

Liar.

The breeze seemed to whisper the word. He walked to the edge of the deck with his coffee, picked up an acorn and tossed it into the woods. A flash of yellow and black caught his eye. Far below he could see the road that ran along the lake and others that cut away from it. A cyclist was already out this morning, no doubt getting a punishing workout on the area's many steep inclines. He watched the rider slip in and out of view as the road curved and then dipped briefly before sloping up. A woman, he thought, although from this distance she looked more like a bumblebee. He sipped his coffee and contemplated going for a ride himself. He could use the workout. Perhaps an hour or so on his bike would help him forget about Claire. Nothing else had.

The rider came to a turnoff, but instead of heading down toward town, she began the ascent. Definitely a woman, he decided. Too small to be a man and he doubted a teenaged boy would be out this early on a school morning.

Ethan raised his nearly empty coffee mug to her in salute.

"Gutsy move, sweetheart," he murmured, then chuckled. "But you're going to regret the impulse in about another eighth of a mile."

Sure enough, she slowed a moment later, but she didn't stop and start walking her bike as he'd figured she would. Ethan knew his quads would be burning mercilessly by that point in the journey. She kept going, though. Her progress was slow and almost painful to watch. He lost sight of her for a moment behind a thicket of evergreens and figured she'd either decided to turn back or had ended her ride at one of the cottages along the lower part of the ridge, and so he got up to refill his coffee cup. When he came back out a moment later, though, she was just down the ridge, cutting up the steep hillside on the sparsely traveled two-track that became a private road.

His private road.

It would take the rider several minutes to reach him. She would be in first gear, he thought, pedaling for all she was worth at this point, even though she was barely moving faster than if she were walking. Still, Ethan was impressed. He'd never managed to conquer that hill without stopping at least twice, maybe three times…and swearing a lot more frequently than that, he admitted to himself on a chuckle.

He could get a better look at her now, although she wore a helmet and wraparound sunglasses and her head was lowered in concentration, making it hard to see the rest of her face. Her hair was short, but brown ends curled from beneath the headgear to graze the back of a slim neck. She was on the small side in both height and build, but definitely athletic given what she had just accomplished.

When she hit the stretch of road that leveled off just in front of his home, Ethan walked to the steps that led down to the driveway. She wore a yellow nylon jacket over black pants that elongated her legs and fit snugly over thighs that were muscular but no less feminine. The little jolt of lust he experienced surprised him, as did the fact that his hands wanted to roam where his mind seemed determined to wander.

He used one to wave instead. "Good morning."

"'Mornin'," she huffed out.

He wasn't acquainted with everyone in the area, but he didn't recognize this woman. Oddly, something about her seemed familiar.

"Hell of a ride up that hill," he commented conversationally.

He saw her head bob in response, but she didn't say anything. Her chest was rising and falling…rising and falling…rising and falling as she sucked in air. He was staring at her breasts through the tight-fitting jacket, he realized, and ordered himself to stop.

"Do I need to call paramedics?" he called out, striving to keep it light.

"N-no." She dismounted the bike, lowered the

kickstand and then bent at her waist to brace her gloved hands on her knees. "Just need…to catch… my…breath."

His memory stirred at the smoky tone. His heart stopped. For just a moment there she'd sounded like Claire. But that was ridiculous. His ex-wife wouldn't just show up at his vacation home in Glen Arbor. She was merely on his mind since he'd recently spoken to her, dreamed about her. He studied the woman for another moment. No, not Claire. Definitely not Claire. She had been far slighter in build and certainly not the type to take on challenges, physical or otherwise. She left that to others.

Ethan relaxed. "Well, when you do, come up on the deck and have a seat. A ride like that deserves a reward. I've got coffee or orange juice if you'd prefer."

The offer of refreshments caught Claire off guard, as did Ethan's friendly greeting. She hadn't expected him to be happy to see her, but apparently he was taking her surprise appearance in his stride. That wouldn't last long once he heard what she'd come to say, she figured. For the moment, however, she savored the truce as she surreptitiously studied him over the top of her sunglasses. He looked terrific. It was just her luck that the photograph hadn't done him justice.

"Juice. Thanks."

He nodded and walked inside. When he was gone, Claire straightened, pulled off the helmet and did her best to fluff her matted hair. It was probably a wasted effort, she decided, pushing the sunglasses on to the top of her head and using them to hold her hair off her forehead and out of her eyes. Her leg muscles were still tight and twitching as she climbed a trio of steps and stood at the railing of Ethan's deck.

Under other circumstances she might have admired the stunning panoramic view. But she was too keyed up, too rattled by seeing him again. She hadn't expected to feel this ridiculously flustered and self-conscious.

In truth, she hadn't planned to come here at all this morning when she'd started out on her ride just after dawn. She'd been in Glen Arbor for more than twenty-four hours, working up her nerve to confront him and explain the situation with the diary. E-mails from Simone assured her that nothing had leaked out…yet.

She was staying at a bed-and-breakfast in town, a quaint two-story farmhouse that dated to the turn of the twentieth century but had all of the modern conveniences guests expected. The bike was borrowed, as were the clothes. After Claire had mentioned to the bed-and-breakfast owner that she wished she'd brought her bike along, the woman had generously offered Claire the loan of her own twenty-one-speed.

Once she'd begun the ride up the ridge, Claire hadn't been able to stop pushing herself. She knew Ethan's home was at the top. She hadn't figured he would be awake or outside this early in the day. But then she'd spied the man sitting on the deck in the chilly morning air. Could it be? Was it him? Curiosity had compelled her at first. Then, when she'd been sure it was Ethan, the only thought in her head, her only goal, had been reaching him.

She was regretting the impulse now. Claire had enough vanity that she'd wanted to look her best for their first face-to-face encounter in years. Chilly though it was, she was perspiring and she didn't need a mirror to know her hair was a mess, her makeup minimal and, while the clothes she'd borrowed fit reasonably well, the close-fitting synthetic fabrics would not have been her choice of attire.

She heard the sliding glass door open and her heart began to pound anew. Soon enough the bomb would have to be dropped and this fragile peace would shatter.

"I suppose I should confess that I've never made it to the top without stopping a few times," Ethan was saying.

Claire turned, smiling at his admission. One of the things she'd always liked about him was that he could give credit where it was due. He didn't have to be better than everyone else. His ego could withstand being bested, even by a woman. That was not the case for most of the men in her family's elite social circle.

"When did you take up riding?"

"About four y—" He broke off abruptly. The easygoing smile he'd been wearing slipped away and his lips flattened into an unwelcoming line. Stunned, that was what he was. And a good one hundred and eighty degrees from happy.

"My God! It *is* you."

The realization that he hadn't recognized her landed like a boxer's quick jab. "Yes, it's me."

"What are you doing here?" The words came out as a demand rather than a question. He tossed the juice he'd brought outside for her over the deck's railing and set the glass on one of the low tables with a snap. His offer of refreshment had obviously been withdrawn.

Claire swallowed and the dryness in her mouth had nothing to do with her recent exertion. "I needed to see you, Ethan."

"And I made it clear I didn't want to see you."

"Which is why I decided just to show up."

"The end justifies the means?"

She nodded slowly. "In this case."

"From my experience with you, I'd say that's true in every case."

"Ethan—"

"You always get what you want," he spat.

She didn't like the way he made her sound: manipulative, devious. Spoiled.

"No. I don't always get what I want."

He folded his arms over his chest. "You're trespassing."

Claire refused to be cowed. She crossed her arms as well. "Yes."

His frown intensified. "I'd like you to leave."

"And I will. In a minute."

"Now."

She canted one leg out to the side and studied him. No, indeed. The picture on his Web site hadn't done him justice. The professional head shot had only hinted at broad shoulders and a powerful build. And it hadn't revealed a thing about his stubborn disposition.

"You used to be more reasonable," she told him.

Surprise flickered momentarily in his gaze. Then he said, "I'm still reasonable."

"Not from where I'm standing."

"Then why don't you come a little closer?" he suggested silkily.

The words raised gooseflesh on Claire's arms, even though they sounded more like a threat than a dare. "That's okay. I'm not nearsighted. You must be, though. I take it you didn't recognize me."

He snorted. "Not in the least or I would have hollered for you to turn around before you'd made it halfway up the ridge."

Claire merely shrugged. "I probably would have continued anyway." He wasn't the only one who could be stubborn.

"It's the hair." He motioned to her head. "What in the hell did you do to it?"

"Cut it," she replied, reaching up to tug at the ends brushing her nape.

"It's short."

"It's easy."

"It used to hide your eyes, your face," he said.

"It can't any longer. I don't need it to."

He frowned before exhaling sharply. She thought she heard him swear. "Say what's on your mind and go."

She swallowed, deciding to keep it brief and to the

point. "First, I'd like to start with another apology for my past behavior. I didn't have a spine, so I thought I could borrow yours."

"Use, you mean."

"Use." There was that unpalatable word again. But she agreed with a brisk nod. "Anyway, I'll apologize again for that, even though I don't think you're in the mood to accept it."

She noted the folded arms, the hard set of his mouth.

"You have no idea what I'm in the mood for, Claire." And though she doubted he meant it to, his gaze dipped down, lingered for a scant moment on her breasts, before jerking away.

"W-well, even though I am sorry, it's not the reason I'm here."

"Just how did you find me?" he asked.

"That's not really important. Something has come up since we spoke the other day."

His dark brows tugged together. "What could come up? And what could it possibly have to do with me? There's nothing between us, Claire, unless you count bad memories."

Was that all? She almost said the words aloud. But she caught herself and asked, "Have you ever mentioned our marriage to anyone?"

"Why in the hell would I?" He snorted. "It's not exactly something I'm eager to admit to people. I'm sure you've kept your mouth shut too. It would have been awfully embarrassing to admit to your fiancé."

"My fiancé?"

"Excuse me. I guess he would be your husband now. Or is he another ex?"

Claire stared at him in confusion. "Who are you talking about?"

"Ashton."

"Ashton…Beaumont?" she asked, her mind stretching back through the years to come up with the last name.

"What, you were engaged to another Ashton when you married me?"

"I was never engaged to Ashton Beaumont," she replied.

"Never?" Ethan's tone and raised eyebrows turned the question into a taunt.

"Never. Ashton wanted to marry me," she admitted. "We dated for a while and he proposed the Christmas before you and I met."

"And you turned him down?" Ethan's expression made it clear he didn't believe her.

"There was a lot of pressure on me at the time to accept his proposal. My parents felt it would be a good match. So did the Beaumonts." She laughed without humor then. "I think Ashton and I were the only two who weren't completely convinced. But, yes, I turned him down."

"So why would your father tell me that you were engaged?" he challenged.

Claire hadn't seen that one coming. She blinked in surprise, her mouth falling open before she could form a coherent response.

"My father told you that? When?" she asked.

"When do you think?"

"Vegas." It came out a whisper.

Sumner could be high-handed and manipulative, but it still shocked her to discover he would lie outright and use any means necessary to get his way.

As angry and hurt as she was to learn of her father's duplicity, Ethan's behavior wounded her more deeply.

"And you believed him?"

He shifted his weight to his other foot, the only sign that her question might have struck a nerve. "You'd gone to pack your bags, Claire. So, yeah, I believed him."

"I'm not proud of my behavior, Ethan. And I'm not here now to make excuses for it."

"You married me to get out of a sticky situation. Not many excuses can be made for that."

Had that been the only reason? After all, she hadn't married Ashton, no matter how many times her father had lectured her or her mother had taken to her bed. Standing in front of Ethan now with her emotions swirling and attraction sizzling, she was sure of only one thing: "I married *you*."

"And then you divorced me."

"As I recall, that was pretty mutual. You didn't put up a fight."

"Did you want me to?" he shot back.

Yes. But then she recalled the check she'd seen in his hand and she shook her head. "When you get right down to it, we really didn't know one another."

Ethan watched her, still unable to believe it was really Claire standing before him and not a figment of his fertile imagination or a remnant of those arousing dreams he'd had.

She was the same, but different. *I've changed.* She'd told him that on the telephone. He hadn't believed her. He still didn't believe that deep down, where it counted, she'd undergone a major transformation from the selfish, self-absorbed woman she'd been. But on the surface, she was undisputedly new.

And improved, he decided, noting the toned physique, the confident way she stood with her shoulders back, her chin up, her gaze direct and just this side of challenging.

He wasn't sure about the short hair yet. Long, it had been beautiful, sexy. He recalled how it had looked fanned out on a pillow. He remembered how it had felt fisted in his hands as he'd tipped over the edge of sanity and taken her with him.

"Let's skip this stroll down memory lane," he snapped irritably. "You mentioned that something has come up."

"Yes." She appeared nervous suddenly. Her gaze cut away and she fidgeted with the Velcro fasteners on the backs of the cycling gloves. "I made a couple of good friends during a recent trip. Certain things came out about our pasts. Things we'd done. Things we regretted and wanted to make right."

Hence the apology, he thought. "Go on."

"One of my friends wrote everything down in her diary. Including names."

Ethan's sense of dread worsened. "My name?"

"Yes. I mentioned our brief marriage, our subsequent divorce." She cleared her throat. "I told them about the check my father gave you."

"I didn't know you knew about that."

"I did."

"It was a hefty sum," Ethan replied bitterly. He could have done a lot with that kind of money had he cashed it. Instead, he'd folded it up and kept it all these years in his wallet as a reminder to follow his head rather than his heart.

"Was I worth it?" Claire asked.

"What?"

"Never mind." She waved a hand and he saw her swallow. "Getting back to the point of this conversation, the diary in which all of this information was written has fallen into the hands of a journalist."

"A journalist!" he shouted.

"He's not American. He's Australian and he's done nothing with the information at this point," she added, as if trying to reassure him. It didn't make him feel any better.

"But he could."

Claire nodded, exhaled. "He could."

"And if that happens, it's a good bet the American press would pick up the story given how well-known the Mayfield name is."

"Yes."

Ethan felt his blood pressure rise. "And that brings us back to me."

"Seaver Security Solutions has been featured in a national business journal and various newspaper articles."

Ethan interrupted. "But this might make for more interesting headlines."

She nodded again. "Especially if the media factor in the tie to Mayfield."

Ethan raked a hand through his hair. The timing couldn't be lousier. This was the last thing he needed while trying to woo a high-caliber investor. "Let me get this straight. You and a couple of gal pals were lounging around some vacation resort, running off your mouths about your pasts. One of you jotted down the particulars, including my name, in some diary, which then somehow found its way into the hands of a reporter."

She seemed about to argue with his assessment of the facts, but then nodded. "More or less. I'm sorry."

Ethan swore and stalked to where she stood at the rail. "*Sorry?* You're *sorry?*" he demanded, grabbing her by the shoulders and giving her a little shake to emphasize his words. "It keeps coming back to that, doesn't it, Claire?"

It kept coming back to her.

He was angry, he told himself. She'd used him. She'd hurt him. She could wind up ruining him.

Even knowing that wasn't enough to prevent what happened next because, when he heard her breath hitch, he found himself sucked back in, wanting to sample again what he'd savored a lifetime ago.

He lowered his head in jerky increments, waiting for self-restraint that never manifested itself. When their mouths were mere inches apart it was Claire who closed the distance. She leaned in, bringing their bodies close enough to bump, and their lips brushed together. He could feel the heat radiating from her. It all but engulfed him when she raised her arms to grip his shoulders and began to kiss him in earnest.

She was better at it than he remembered, or at least than he had allowed himself to remember. It ticked him off. As did the fact that she felt so damned good in his arms, perfect in a way no other woman had since he'd last held Claire.

"I've wanted to hate you," he whispered against her cheek as his mouth moved from her lips to the sensitive skin just below her ear.

A moan vibrated from her throat and the hands that had been on his shoulders were now moving over his back. "I know."

She sounded as if she understood exactly how he'd felt back then…and now. She hadn't a clue.

"You can't know." He spat the words angrily as he started down her neck, his teeth grazing the soft skin. "You—"

The rest of his tirade was lost when he felt cold fingers dip beneath the hem of his thick fleece pullover. They didn't stay at the small of his back. They trailed boldly to the front, stopping just above the snap of his jeans.

This was insane. He needed to put an end to it. He needed…more.

Ethan leaned away far enough so he could reach the zipper at the front of her jacket. He lowered it with one brutal yank, before shoving it down her shoulders. Beneath it, Claire wore a snug-fitting black T-shirt. The air was cold and her nipples strained against the light-weight fabric, which was slightly damp from her perspiration. He swore he saw steam waft from her torso as she leaned back against the deck railing, tacitly granting him greater access.

He had the hem hiked up halfway to her breasts, exposing some very toned abdominal muscles, when he came to his senses. With a vile curse he staggered back. A good five feet separated the two of them—five feet, ten years and more memories than he generally cared to recall. Ethan scrubbed the back of his hand over his mouth and held on to the most bitter of them now.

"You're not the only one with regrets, Claire."

He might as well have slapped her. Claire straightened and pulled the sides of her jacket together, mortified by what had just happened. More mortified by the disappointment she felt at what hadn't. Gathering up the remnants of her dignity—a paltry sum at that point—she managed a shaky nod.

"I know."

"I know, I know," Ethan mimicked. "Like hell you do."

He swore again and paced to the far end of the deck. His back was turned to her, but she remembered quite vividly the condition of his front.

"Wh-what are you going to do about the publicity

threat?" she asked, deciding it best to change the subject. "It probably would be a good idea to have a plan in place for damage control."

He glared at her over one shoulder. "I don't think I need advice from you on how to address this matter given that your actions are the reason I find myself in this position to begin with."

He sounded a little too much like her father just then—dismissive, discounting her thoughts on any given matter. As much as his rejection a moment earlier had, that wounded.

"I guess not."

It began to rain. Claire glanced up at the sky, which had darkened considerably since her arrival. It was a fitting accompaniment to her bleak mood. She pulled the sunglasses from the top of her head and tucked them into the pocket of her borrowed jacket. She wouldn't need them for the ride back.

"I should be going."

Ethan snorted. "So soon?"

She ignored the sarcasm. "I'm staying in town at the Cloverleaf Bed & Breakfast if you need to reach me for anything."

He turned, frowned. "You're staying?"

"Yes."

"For how long?"

The rain was coming down harder now. Already her hair was wet and she realized she was shivering even as parts of her body remained on fire. The downhill ride to the bed-and-breakfast would be tricky, possibly even dangerous if the temperature dipped any lower and ice formed. Claire didn't care. For some reason she couldn't quite put her finger on, she was feeling reckless.

"Another day or two. I'm sure we'll know something shortly. We can address it as a unified force if necessary, call a press conference or whatever."

She walked to where she'd left the twenty-one-speed and put on the helmet, securing the strap before mounting the bike. "I'll be in touch."

Ethan stood in the rain and watched her go. Damn her! Claire had done it again. She had managed to turn his life upside down in a matter of days.

The potential public relations nightmare for Seaver was the least of it. He rubbed a hand over his mouth again, but he was unable to wipe away the memory of that kiss. He resented that. He resented her. But he was honest enough to admit to himself that as much as he wished it were otherwise, he still wanted her.

An hour later, freshly showered and dressed in dry clothes, Ethan hopped in his SUV and headed into town. He wasn't worried about Claire. He wasn't checking up on her or anything. But she'd been noticeably shivering and the roads were rain-slicked. He drove the route he knew she would have taken just to be sure she'd gotten back safely. The last thing he needed right now was for her to land in the hospital.

The bike she'd been riding was parked on the side

porch of the bed-and-breakfast. The jacket he'd levered down her shoulders hung over the rail next to a pair of black pants. Ethan slowed down before he realized what he was doing. When the car behind him honked impatiently, he sped up and continued past.

He was recalling that kiss, he realized. And he'd thought an erotic dream had been hard to recover from.

No matter. Claire would be gone in a day or two and, assuming their marriage and divorce remained secret, he wasn't likely to see her again. That was what he wanted. Claire gone and everything about her past tense.

CHAPTER FOUR

THE GOOD EATS Gallery & Grill in Glen Arbor boasted homemade bread, freshly caught Great Lakes perch and some of the best pesto this side of Italy. Original paintings by local artists decorated the walls of the small establishment and fresh flowers sprouted from old olive oil bottles on the cloth-covered tabletops.

It was quaint and quietly upscale, with a menu that would have done a cordon bleu-trained chef proud. Yet all of its dishes were served on unpretentious stoneware.

Claire had little doubt that in the summer—or even a few weeks ago when the fall color had been at its peak—the place would have been packed with patrons and calling ahead for a reservation would have been a must. This time of year, however, she had the restaurant to herself now that an older couple had paid their bill and were heading out the door.

"How are you enjoying your stay in Glen Arbor?" the waitress had asked her when she'd delivered Claire's meal a few minutes earlier.

The short answer was: Claire wasn't. She was on tenterhooks, wondering if Ethan would call, checking her e-mail for word from Simone, and waiting for an elusive *something* that made it all but impossible to sleep at night no matter how tired she was.

"The scenery is beautiful," Claire had evaded.

And it was. Another time, in another frame of mind, the turquoise lakes, undulating countryside and charming array of shops might have caused her to lengthen her stay, despite the fact that the leaves had dropped and the air held a bite. But it really made no sense to linger now. She had things she could do back in Chicago, career plans to make and an apartment to decorate. And so she was leaving. She'd made arrangements to fly out later that day.

Claire picked at her salad and mulled over the e-mail she'd received from Simone. Her friend had assured Claire that nothing had broken in the media yet but she was still unsure as to whether she could trust this journalist, Ryan Tanner.

Something about the way Simone described the man in her e-mails made Claire curious. Simone didn't like him. That much came through loud and clear. Still…

Belle, who had been strangely incommunicado, had finally weighed in on the matter. She didn't care what Ryan Tanner decided to do with their information, as her post had indicated with enough pith to make Claire's lips pucker.

She'd written:

Ivo knows everything. So, as far as I'm concerned, you can tell Ryan Tanner to publish and be
damned.

Belle had ended her note with:

Not so easy for you, Claire.

No, not so easy.

Of course, her friends had also offered their insights
into Ethan's rather vehement reaction to Claire's arrival
in Glen Arbor and her two attempts to apologize.
Simone had written:

Do you think he could still have feelings for you?

Oh, sure he did. That much was obvious. Ethan
loathed her. He wished he'd never met her. Certainly he
wished he'd never married her.

You're not the only one with regrets, Claire.

Belle, as usual, had cut right to the heart of the matter
with a different question:

What exactly are your feelings for him?

Claire hadn't written back. She wasn't sure of the
answer. She pondered it now as she rooted through
vinaigrette-coated mixed greens for the last of the dried
cherries. She'd felt fairly certain of her emotions when

she'd left Chicago mere days ago. She had chalked up her sense of anticipation to nostalgia and nerves. After all, it was only natural for a woman to have a certain sentimental attachment and attraction to the first man with whom she'd made love.

That had worked right up until Ethan had kissed her.

Claire hadn't been pulled back in time as much as she had been thrust forward, past the here and now and into the future. That kiss had started her wondering where she would be, where she *wanted* to be, in a year, two years, ten. And not just professionally. It had started her wondering whom her life would include.

The door opened and a woman breezed into the restaurant along with a chilly gust of air. She was blonde, long-legged and, when she took off her coat, obviously pregnant. She smiled at Claire as the hostess directed her to a nearby table.

"It's getting cold out there," Claire said conversationally.

"Yes, very." The woman rubbed her hands together as she settled into her seat. "The forecasters are even predicting a chance of snow by the weekend."

"I saw on the news that they got a couple inches last night in Chicago," Claire replied. "That's where I'm from."

"Really? My husband is originally from Chicago. We don't get back there much these days. Most of his family has moved to Michigan now."

The bed-and-breakfast owner had mentioned that a lot of people with summer homes in the area came not just from downstate but from the surrounding states as well. Even so, the fine hairs on the back of Claire's neck began to tingle. No, couldn't be, she chided herself. The waitress came over with a menu then and ended all speculation.

"Hello, Mrs. Seaver. Good to see you again. Can I get you something to drink?"

Claire's salad fork clattered on the wooden floor. *Mrs Seaver?* Just yesterday Ethan had kissed Claire with enough passion to leave her yearning for much more and the jerk was *married?* She wasn't sure which emotion she felt more intensely: shock or anger. Shock won, but only because it was the more straightforward of the two. Anger had too many dangerous currents eddying below its surface to make it safe to mull over.

Even before that kiss, she had never considered the possibility that Ethan had remarried after their divorce, much less that his wife could be expecting a child. The brief biography on his Web site hadn't mentioned a family but, for all she knew, he had children, sandy-haired boys with mischief glowing in their green eyes, cherub-faced girls with their daddy's determination.

"Will anyone be joining you?" the waitress asked the woman.

"My husband should be here any minute and I think my brother-in-law is coming too."

If Claire hadn't already dropped her fork, she would have then. My cue to leave, she thought, blotting her mouth and then laying the napkin aside. She was no coward, but nor was she eager to find herself in the middle of an unpleasant domestic situation. She wanted to be gone before Ethan arrived and found himself in a room with one wife too many.

Ex-wife, she reminded herself. She was his ex legally and in every other way. That fact made the possibility of an encounter no easier to stomach.

"I'll bring you a new fork in a moment," the waitress said as she passed Claire on her way to the kitchen.

"That's okay. I've finished eating. I'll take my check, please."

"Sure thing." The young woman pulled it from the pocket of her starched apron and handed it to Claire. "I can take that up to the register as soon as you're ready."

Claire decided not to wait until the waitress returned for it. Pay and go quickly, that was her plan. She left enough money on the tabletop to cover her lunch plus provide a very generous tip and was struggling into her coat when the door opened.

It was firearm deer season in Michigan. Claire knew this because she had heard gunshots her first evening in town and had asked the bed-and-breakfast owner about them. As Ethan stepped over the threshold Claire thought she now understood how those animals must feel to find themselves trapped in the crosshairs, seconds from doom. Part of her wanted to bound away and put as much distance as possible between the pair of them, but that was no longer a possibility. He had easily spotted her in the small, nearly empty restaurant and the open, friendly expression he'd been wearing became guarded before turning hard.

Claire raised her chin and started toward the door. Unfortunately, this brought her directly into his path. Instead of stepping aside, he maintained his ground. She did as well. Pushing back her short hair, she tipped back her head and held his gaze.

"Hello, Ethan."

"Claire. I figured you'd left town already."

"Figured or hoped?" When he merely smiled, she said, "Don't worry, I'll be leaving shortly."

"Good." He jingled a set of keys in one hand before stowing it in his pocket. "Any word on…that public relations matter we discussed yesterday?"

She shook her head. "None."

He expelled a breath. "Well, no news is good news, I guess."

"I think so."

Ethan glanced past Claire then and, apparently spotting the restaurant's other occupant, waved. That didn't bother Claire so much as his accompanying smile. The anger she'd decided not to delve into a moment earlier swirled once more and sucked her in. It turned her tone crisp when she added, "By the way, let me offer my belated congratulations."

His expression wary, Ethan asked, "For what exactly?"

Claire tilted her head discreetly in the other woman's direction, raising her eyebrows even as she lowered her voice. "When your hands were busily trying to get beneath my shirt yesterday I didn't think to look for a ring, so you'll have to excuse me for failing to realize you were married. And expecting a child."

She figured that blunt statement would elicit some remorse or at the very least a suitable amount of embarrassment. One side of his mouth lifted in a cocky grin instead.

"Do you remember where your hands were at the time?"

Because Claire did, exactly, she decided to end their conversation. Stepping around him, she said, "Goodbye."

But Ethan followed her to the door. "I don't believe I owe you any explanations, Claire."

"No. Your wife—*second wife*—would be the one who deserves those," she said, keeping her voice just above a whisper. She shook her head. "I have to tell you, though, I'm a little disappointed. You didn't strike me as the sort of man who would … stray."

"And you didn't strike me as a manipulative, self-serving liar, but there you go." He shrugged as he said it, but his gaze had turned hard once again.

Claire reined in her temper. His words reminded her of the purpose of her visit to Glen Arbor. It took an effort, but she managed a more conciliatory tone when she said, "I'm glad everything has worked out so well for you."

His eyes narrowed. "You know, you almost sound like you mean that."

"I do." Or at least she wanted to. She swallowed.

"You have a successful business and…a family. I remember how much you wanted both."

An unreadable emotion flickered briefly in his eyes just before he snorted out a laugh. "I'd forgotten how I blathered on about that during one of our first dates. Sorry if I bored you at the time."

"You never bored me, Ethan." It was easy to sound sincere because she meant it. "You had so much determination, so much resolve. I envied that, admired it. You made me want to be…more."

"I don't know what to say to that," he admitted slowly.

"You don't have to say anything." She coughed, embarrassed. "Now, I'll let you join your wife."

"About that. Claire—"

She raised a hand to silence him. "No. You might not believe me, but I do want you to be happy, Ethan. Really." Of course that didn't stop her from offering some pointed advice. "Word to the wise, though, you might not be able to manage marital bliss if you go around kissing other women."

"You didn't use to be so outspoken," he remarked, not the least bit offended.

She took his assessment as a compliment. "I didn't use to be a lot of things, Ethan. What can I say? I've changed."

His eyes narrowed. "So, you want me to be happy."

"Yes."

"And you traveled all the way to Glen Arbor just to tell me that you're sorry."

She nodded. "Well, that and to let you know about the not so little matter of my friend's missing diary."

When he continued to frown at her, Claire said, "I'd better go. Goodbye, Ethan."

She was proud of herself. The exchange had been dignified, civilized. She dismissed the disappointment that she still didn't feel the overwhelming sense of relief or resolution she'd hoped to experience. Perhaps that would come later.

She glanced over his shoulder at the woman who was sipping tea and eyeing Claire with frank interest. She couldn't resist adding, "And good luck. I think you're going to have some explaining to do."

Then she pulled open the door, stepped past a man who was just on the other side of it, and walked away.

Ethan watched Claire go. Much like that kiss yesterday, their conversation just now had left him confused— among other things.

"Who was that?" his brother asked after he entered the restaurant. "Do you know her?"

"I'm not really sure." Ethan meant it, just as he meant it when he added, "But I intend to find out."

The woman walked fast, her stride brisk and purposeful, her shoulders back and her head up despite the stinging slap of the wind coming in off the great lake. Ethan had to run to catch up to her.

"Claire!"

She stopped, turned at the sound of his voice. The breeze tugged at the short ends of her hair, pulling it this way and that and giving him a clear view of her expression. She looked surprised that he'd come after her and it made him wonder, just for a moment, if she would have been equally surprised—maybe even pleased?—had he come after her all those years earlier.

Now that they were face-to-face, Ethan had no idea what he planned to say or why he felt the need to say anything. He shoved his hands deep into the pockets of his leather jacket and searched for the right words. The ones that tumbled out in an uncharacteristically disjointed fashion were, "She's not my wife. Laura. You know, the woman in the restaurant. She's my sister-in-law. She's married to the man who came in just as you were leaving. James. That was James. You never met him. James. My brother. The youngest."

She nodded and kicked at the gravel with the tip of her shoe, making him believe she felt just as awkward. "So, you don't have a family?"

"No. I've never married." He swallowed. "Again, that is."

Her head tilted to one side and she inquired, "Once burned, twice shy?"

Ethan didn't like the sound of that, so he said, "Nah. Just been waiting for the right time and the right person." He pulled his hands out of his pockets and tugged the zipper on his jacket closer to his chin. "What about you?"

"I guess I've been waiting too."

Their gazes locked as memories stirred.

"…You're the one, Claire. You're the one I've been

waiting for." He'd pushed the long hair back from her eyes, kissed her cheek. "It's crazy, probably too soon, but I love you."

She'd risen up on tiptoe to kiss him in earnest. Then she'd said, "Let's get married. Now. Fly to Vegas. Why should we wait?..."

Ethan looked away and rubbed his chilled hands together. "I can't imagine that sits well with Sumner."

"Not particularly, no, but I've given up on pleasing my parents."

His brows rose and his gaze snapped back. "Have you finally figured out that that's not possible?"

"No. I can make them happy. What I figured out is that it's not possible for me to live my own life if I do that." She cleared her throat, looking a little embarrassed. Then she scuffed the ground again. "So, does this mean you accept my apology?"

"I want to." The reply's ambiguity came as a surprise to both of them.

"You still can't forgive me."

Ethan didn't care for the serious turn their conversation had taken. Nor did he care for the memories it had stoked to life. "It was a long time ago."

"Well, truce, then?"

"We haven't been at war, Claire."

"What have we been?"

Waiting. The word whispered through his mind again. He shook his head and decided to change the subject. "You mentioned you were leaving."

"Yes. Today." She pulled up the sleeve of her coat and glanced at her watch, a slim little number that was no less pricy for its meager proportions. "My flight departs in about five hours."

He dug his wallet from his back pocket and pulled out a business card, which he handed to her. "Well, if anything comes up regarding the diary, call the cell phone number."

"Okay." She pocketed the card. "Do you want my cell number?"

He was shaking his head before she finished the sentence. "No need. If for some reason I need to contact you, I'll call the Mayfield offices in Chicago."

"You won't get me. I no longer work there."

Ethan wasn't sure he'd heard her right. "What do you mean? Did you transfer to another site?"

"No. I quit a few days ago," she said.

He whistled. "I have to admit, that surprises me. I mean, talk about job security."

"I had job security," she agreed with a stiff nod. "But I wanted more than that."

Ethan frowned. "Such as?"

"A promotion, specifically to vice president in charge of product development in North America."

He studied her for a moment, torn between admiration and derision. "That's a key position with a lot of responsibility."

"Exactly why I wanted it," she informed him.

"I take it Sumner doesn't think you're qualified."

Claire winced visibly before regrouping. "No, he

doesn't. But I am." She snorted. "Far more so than the guy who's going to get it."

"Maybe he needs the paycheck more."

Far from being insulted by his allusion to her wealth, she rolled her eyes. "Oh, please. Is that how you determine your employees' promotions? Net worth doesn't strike me as a great predictor of talent."

Ethan shrugged, though, of course she was right. But he wasn't done needling her. "You know, you go to work somewhere else and you won't be the boss's daughter."

Her eyes narrowed. "What's that supposed to mean?"

"Just that no one's going to feel the need to walk on eggshells around you."

"I can pull my own weight. And as I recall, you never walked on eggshells around me," she reminded him.

Indeed, he hadn't. "I didn't give a damn about your last name, Claire. The fact that you were a high-and-mighty Mayfield wasn't part of the attraction."

"Oh? What was the attraction?"

The blunt question threw him off balance, allowing more of the memories he'd kept buried to surface. What was the attraction? *The way you used to look at me. The way you listened, giving me your undivided attention. The way you seemed to believe in me even when the odds were long. The way you'd sigh after I kissed you as if you'd never been so well loved.*

Ethan cleared his throat. "I liked your butt." He punctuated the off-color compliment with a shrug even though he was feeling anything but nonchalant.

Claire wasn't put off, though. Her smile bloomed. "Same goes."

Ethan moved closer, cutting the space between them to a stingy gap. If he lowered his head, he could kiss her. If he lifted his hands, he could settle them on her waist. A car drove by and leaves swirled around their feet. To everything there was a season, Ethan thought. And the season for him and Claire had passed. He stepped back.

"Well, take care." He started to turn, but she stopped him.

"Oh! I almost forgot. I have something of yours I want to return." She motioned toward the bed-and-breakfast, which was just up ahead on the same side of the road. "It's in my suitcase. Got a minute?"

He needed to get away from her, put some distance between them physically and emotionally. "Sure," he said.

Claire hurried ahead. Ethan followed at a slower pace. She'd already disappeared inside when he reached the porch, so he settled his hip on the railing and waited, happy to have a moment alone to get his riled emotions in check. Still, he couldn't help wondering: What did she have of his? What would she hold on to all of these years?

The door opened and she stepped out. The mystery would soon be solved. The scarred boards of the porch creaked when he stood. Claire smiled awkwardly and moistened her lips.

"Here."

Ethan held out his hand and she dropped something on to his palm. It took him a moment to realize that it was the wedding band he'd placed on her finger in Vegas. He closed his fist around it.

"You kept this?" His throat had gone tight so his voice was just above a whisper. To compensate, he summoned up a cocky half smile. "It's not worth much, you know. It's not like it's a family heirloom or anything. You didn't need to return it."

"I felt I did."

He tucked the ring in his pocket. "Fine. Thanks."

"Well, goodbye." She reached behind her, opening the door even as she spoke.

She'd already crossed the threshold when he managed to say, "Goodbye, Claire."

Ethan sat on the beach in Empire watching the waves batter the shore. Lake Michigan was in a black mood and so was he.

He blamed Claire for that. Now, instead of just wanting her, he found himself wanting to respect her. Wanting to like her. Not a good sign. No, not a good sign at all. Physical attraction he could handle. After all, it was only natural for a man to be drawn to a beautiful woman. That was why sexy models were used to sell everything from men's cologne to cars. But this was threatening to snowball into something beyond simple lust and that made him edgy.

Ethan pulled the ring from his pocket. It was cheap, gold-plated. Hell, get right down to it and it was one step above tin. Yet she'd kept it. Now she'd returned it.

As he studied the ring, the thought occurred to him: maybe that was what he needed to do to finally purge her from his system. Return something that didn't belong to him. Maybe that would restore his peace once and for all. Rising to his feet, he glanced at his watch. If he hurried, he just might make it.

CHAPTER FIVE

DELAYED.

Claire sighed as she read the monitor at the airport. Her flight would not be leaving on time. Figures, she thought. It had been that kind of a day.

The mission that had brought her to Glen Arbor was complete, but it felt far from accomplished. She was still waiting for the sense of relief, but it was proving elusive. Maybe she just needed to accept that for some acts an apology, no matter how heartfelt, would not be enough. Maybe she needed to accept that "I want to" was as good as it was going to get when it came to gaining Ethan's actual forgiveness.

Overall, his reaction to her appearance had hardly been a surprise. She hadn't expected him to be overjoyed to see her, especially since she'd come bearing unpleasant news about a possible public relations nightmare. Then again, she hadn't expected him to kiss her and make her burn from the remembered heat of their lovemaking.

Just thinking about that kiss now had her body turning boneless. Her shoulders went lax, allowing the strap of her carry-on to slide off. The bag fell to the floor with a thud that did not bode well for the cosmetics inside. She bent down to retrieve it at the same time a man's loafers came into view and a masculine hand shot out.

With her fingers around the strap, Claire straightened and glanced over, a smile forming and a polite thank-you ready to be issued to the would-be good Samaritan. Then she blinked and the bag hit the floor for a second time.

"Ethan!"

"Hi, Claire. I wasn't sure I'd get here before your flight left," he said.

"No problem there." She motioned toward the bank of monitor screens. "Delayed."

"Well, better than canceled."

She nodded. "So, what are you doing here?"

A flight had just arrived and passengers began to stream around them in the small airport.

"Can we go somewhere? Maybe sit down and have a drink or something? I'd like to talk to you."

"Sure."

He lifted the bag, but Claire took it from him and secured the strap on her shoulder. "Thanks, but I can carry it myself."

Ethan watched her for a moment before nodding. With that one simple sentence, more so than anything else she'd said to him, she'd distinguished herself from the old Claire. He'd loved that woman. He'd wanted to protect her and make her happy. It was just his luck that he was starting to like this independent, self-sufficient version better.

They found a booth in the airport's small restaurant. Ethan waited until after they'd ordered a couple of coffees to bring up the reason he'd driven fifteen miles over the posted speed limit the entire way to get to the airport so he could see her before she left.

"I have something I want to return to you too."

The statement had her eyes widening. The lamp hanging over their table caught gold flecks. "Anything I gave you was a gift, Ethan. I certainly don't expect anything back."

"I could say the same thing about the ring."

"That wasn't a gift," she said softly.

"What was it?"

"It was…the symbol of a promise. One made under false pretenses. One I didn't keep."

He was silent for a moment, measuring her words and appreciating their honesty before finally accepting them.

"If you get right down to it, I didn't keep that promise either," he admitted at last.

Claire said nothing, but the gold flecks in her eyes grew brighter with emotions whose meaning he did not want to decipher. As the silence stretched, Ethan coughed.

"Technically, I guess this belongs to your father."

He retrieved the check from his wallet, unfolding the faded slip of paper before handing it to Claire. He watched her expression change from one of curiosity to surprise and then outright disbelief. It wasn't exactly the reaction he'd been expecting.

"Oh, my God! But I thought…" She covered her mouth with one hand and squeezed her eyes shut for a moment. "You didn't cash it."

He frowned. "Of course I didn't cash it. I thought you knew that. Hell, you knew Sumner wrote it. Didn't he tell you? For that matter, didn't you think to ask him or me?"

"I…I…" That was all she managed as she sat there staring at the check and shaking her head.

"You should have asked me. Dammit, Claire, all you had to do was ask." He was angry—at Claire and at the situation. It dissipated somewhat at her forlorn expression when she glanced up.

"It was in your hand when I left," she reminded him. "I thought…you didn't refuse it. You'd always been so determined to make your own way, so when you didn't toss it back in my father's face immediately…"

"Your dad had just dropped the bomb on me about Ashton. Forgive me for being a little off my A-game," he said wryly. Then he swore. "I can't believe you assumed I took it."

"You made assumptions of your own."

He slumped back in his seat. She had him there.

After a moment of silence, Claire said softly, "You didn't cash the check." The sides of her mouth curved.

Ethan straightened. "And you were never engaged to Ashton Beaumont." He felt his own smile starting to emerge, but then it faltered. None of this changed the fact that she'd used him. Or that a decade had passed and they were now different people.

"Attention passengers. Flight 742 to Chicago's Midway Airport will begin boarding momentarily."

The announcement came over the public address system as they stared at one another.

"That's my flight," Claire said.

Ethan nodded. He signaled for their bill, watching his onetime bride as new questions nagged. He mulled over the possible answers as he escorted Claire to the checkpoint. Just before she reached the security desk, she turned.

"Well, it looks like this is goodbye again." She smiled and then her expression sobered. "I'm really glad about the check, Ethan. And I'm sorry—*very* sorry—I thought what I did. I should have known."

"Me too. About Ashton, I mean. At any rate, I should have asked you."

Her smile seemed wistful. "Seems like we could have avoided a lot of unpleasantness if we'd done a better job of communicating."

"Maybe." Ethan rubbed a hand over the back of his neck and found himself wondering if their marriage would have lasted if they had been open and honest with one another from the start. But then he came to one irrefutable fact. "You used me."

"Yes, I did."

"Then I guess none of the miscommunications matter because, when you get right down to it, it was all a lie."

She reached out a hand, rested it on his arm. In a voice barely above a whisper, she admitted, "Not all of it."

In business Ethan relied on gut instinct and prior experience when it came to making tough calls. Taken in combination, they'd never failed him. They seemed to be at odds with one another in this case, though. Let her go, his head said. There was no point in rehashing the past. Ethan decided to go with his gut.

"Do you need to return to Chicago tonight?"

The question had her blinking. "No. I mean, at some point I have to get my résumé together and start looking for a new job. And my apartment needs decorating." She waved a hand. "I recently moved."

"Can all that wait?"

"Wait?" she repeated.

He swallowed. "Yeah, just a day or two."

"I guess it wouldn't hurt to postpone my return for a day…or two," she said slowly. Then, "But I need to know why you're asking, Ethan."

"The short answer?" He laughed nervously. "I'm not sure."

"Well, at least you're decisive." She laughed too, sounding nearly as tense.

"Look, I just think that, given our past, we need to iron this out once and for all." He hoped to God she wouldn't ask what *this* he was referring to, because he didn't know and didn't want to speculate at this point. "We could do that over the phone, but I'd rather do it in person."

That way he could see her expression.

"Are you talking about closure?" she asked as one side of her mouth lifted.

Ethan snorted. "I've never really liked that word, but, yeah, I guess I am."

"We will now begin boarding for Flight 742 to Chicago. Passengers with small children or who require assistance should proceed to the gate."

Claire glanced over her shoulder, her gaze stretching beyond the X-ray machine and metal detector to the passengers who were heading for their destinations. She had a choice of two roads. She knew what awaited her at the end of one. As for the other, she had no idea where it would lead. Even so, when she faced Ethan again she was smiling.

"I happen to be a huge proponent of closure these days. So, yes, I'll stay."

After renting a car, Claire drove back to Glen Arbor, following the taillights of Ethan's Escalade the entire way. She couldn't believe the turn of events. It was almost too much to comprehend.

The check Sumner had written out a decade earlier was in her purse now. She recalled how it looked, dog-eared and nearly severed at the creases, as if Ethan had taken it out often and studied it before refolding and replacing it in his wallet. He'd kept it all of these years and she was pretty sure she knew what it symbolized to him. Her father had thought his new son-in-law could be bought. It shamed Claire to know she'd assumed that too.

Well, now they had a chance to put the past behind them once and for all. This was what she wanted, what she'd hoped for upon her return from the Himalayas. She couldn't wait to contact Belle and Simone with the good news. They were going to be so proud of her. As for Claire, what she felt was… relieved. Yes, that was it. Relieved and invigorated by the prospect of closure at last. She discounted the little quiver of excitement that had her pulse hitching whenever she recalled the way Ethan's voice had sounded when he'd asked her to stay. Under the circumstances, she told herself, anticipation was a perfectly normal state.

She followed Ethan into Glen Arbor. He slowed in front of the bed-and-breakfast, passing the driveway and pulling on to the shoulder of the road. Claire turned in and parked her car. Before leaving the airport, she'd called and reserved her room again. Ethan met her before she'd reached the porch steps. They climbed them together.

"I'm supposed to meet a friend over on South Manitou Island tomorrow morning, but I'll reschedule it." He made a humming noise. "Unless you want to come with me."

The invitation left her flabbergasted. For some reason, it also scared her. It had *tread carefully* written all over it. Claire had never met any of Ethan's friends during their whirlwind courtship.

"Oh, I don't know. I mean, you have plans. No need to rearrange them on account of me. We can meet for dinner." She inwardly flinched. Dinner turned it into a date, so she added a hasty, "Or something."

Ethan stuffed his hands into his trouser pockets and rocked back on his heels. "You're right. I don't know if you could handle it anyway."

She frowned. "What do you mean by that?"

"Just that South Manitou is pretty rustic. No public transportation, no amenities to speak of. There are only a few privately owned cottages left on the island at this point, one of which belongs to my friend's family. It's quite a hike to get to from the boat dock."

She crossed her arms over her chest. "And you don't think I could handle a hike?"

"We're talking miles, Claire."

"I pedaled all the way from here to your home," she reminded him."

"This is hiking, not biking."

"It was mostly uphill." She smiled. "This should pose no problem for me."

"Well, if you think you're up to it," he replied on a shrug.

She thought she caught a glimmer of amusement in his green eyes and so she decided to give as good as she was getting. "I know I'm up for it. One thing has me worried, though."

"What's that?"

She pursed her lips as she eyed his physique. "How much do you weigh?"

"What does that matter?"

"Just trying to figure out if I'll be able to help you limp to safety if something happens to you." She smiled sweetly and Ethan laughed.

"See you in the morning. I'll come by around nine-thirty." He glanced down at her feet and the designer boots she was wearing. "I hope you have something more practical than that in that bag of yours."

"Hmm." Claire grimaced. "Nothing suitable for hiking."

"I'll be here at nine, then. There's a store in town where you can pick up something."

"Okay."

She expected Ethan to leave then, but he didn't. He leaned against the doorjamb instead. The porch light glowed behind him, limning his head in gold. He might have looked like an angel except for the sinful amount of interest brewing in his eyes. She glanced away, worried the same might be visible in hers.

"Have you ever wondered how it might have been between us if we'd stayed married?" he asked.

The question caught her off guard. So much so that she answered with the unvarnished truth. "Can something that intense last?"

"Or does it burn itself out?"

"Uh-huh." She chanced a look at him now and stoked up her courage enough to ask, "Have you reached any conclusions?"

"I used to think I had." He tugged at the short ends

of her hair before tucking them behind one ear. She thought he might kiss her, he'd leaned that close, but he stepped back instead. "Till tomorrow, Claire."

CHAPTER SIX

EARLY THE NEXT morning Claire placed a call to her father.

She'd spoken to her parents once already to let them know where she was. Her father had not been pleased. He'd actually ordered her back to Chicago and threatened to fill the position her resignation had left vacant. Go ahead, she'd told him, when he'd mentioned nothing of reconsidering the promotion.

During this conversation he'd tried another tactic, one that had worked with much greater effectiveness on Claire in the past.

"Your mother is very distraught over your recent behavior. And now running off to see Ethan Seaver," Sumner said. "Her doctor is very concerned about the toll the emotional stress is taking on her overall health."

Claire closed her eyes and counted to ten before replying. "I'm not doing any of this to upset Mother or you for that matter. I needed to do this—all of this—for myself, Dad. Can you understand that?"

"What I understand is that you're being incredibly selfish."

"Selfish! What's selfish about wanting to run my own life? For goodness' sake, Dad, I'm in my thirties! I'm not ten any longer. Or twenty-one," she added meaningfully. That's how old she'd been when she'd married Ethan.

"I did that for your own good," he replied.

"Is that how you justify trying to buy Ethan off? How could you do that, Dad? He was my husband."

"And not a very bright man." Her father snorted. "He never even cashed the check I wrote him."

"I know. I know all about that now." She thought of the well-creased slip of paper and of the proud man who'd had it in his possession all of these years. "It makes me realize that my first impression of him was exactly right. He has integrity and class."

"Class? Have you forgotten that he was a security guard, kitten? He brought in less money in a month than I spend on cigars in a week."

"Yes, and now he's the sole owner of a growing and respected company," she replied. On the other end of the line she thought she heard her father swear.

"You only married him to spite me," Sumner snapped.

"No, Dad, I married him to get away from you." She hadn't meant to say it like that, even though it was the truth.

"Is that a better reason?"

"No, it's not. Not in the least. But the distinction is irrelevant. The fact remains that I used him. I've apologized to him for that. I think we've found a middle ground," she added, thinking about the way Ethan had looked when he'd asked her to stay in Glen Arbor for a couple of days.

"In that case, come home."

"I'll return to Chicago soon enough," she said. "Give Mother my love."

She'd intended to hang up, but her father offered an ominous bit of advice. "Watch yourself, Claire."

"What's that supposed to mean?"

"You used him in the past, have you considered that this time Seaver might be interested in using you?"

"What are you talking about?"

"Just that I've heard he wants to expand his company's research and development capabilities so he can run with the big dogs in the security industry. To do that he'll need a pretty sizable influx of capital."

"You've *heard* this?" She didn't like the sound of that. It implied that her father was trying to insert his hand into her life again. So she asked, "When?"

"Last week." Sure enough, he admitted, "I made some inquiries. I felt it was wise to be informed since I have a vested interest."

"This isn't about you, Dad."

"You're my daughter. That makes it my business. Your bank account—most of which came courtesy of me and your grandfather, don't forget—makes you one of the wealthiest young women in the country, Claire."

"Are you saying my net worth is the only reason a man such as Ethan Seaver would be attracted to me?"

Sumner didn't answer her question. Instead he asked bluntly, "Are you attracted to him?"

The explosive kiss on his porch taunted her, as did the look in Ethan's eyes the evening before when he'd leaned close and tucked her hair behind her ear. But Claire said, "I'm not interested in romance at this point in my life, and neither Ethan nor I is interested in that kind of a relationship."

"A woman of your means needs to watch herself and make a smart alliance," Sumner insisted.

Now there was a cold word for marriage, she thought. "I can assure you, Dad, neither my heart nor my assets are in any danger."

After she hung up, however, Claire wondered whether one might not be just a little more vulnerable than the other.

It was a gorgeous day with the temperature edging close to the fifty degree mark. Claire was dressed in jeans and a thick turtleneck sweater, over which she wore a down vest that Ethan had borrowed from his sister-in-law. Ethan was similarly dressed in jeans and a thick fleece pullover. Dark glasses shaded their eyes from the bright sun.

They both were wearing hiking boots. Ethan had helped Claire pick out a pair at a store in Glen Arbor before they'd set out for nearby Leland. There was no ferry service on this late November day, so a boat had been chartered to take them to South Manitou Island. On the short drive to the dock Ethan offered a brief history of the island.

"According to a Chippewa Indian legend, a bear and her two cubs swam across Lake Michigan to escape a great forest fire in Wisconsin. Mishe Mokwa— that was the mother bear's name—reached the shore of Michigan and rested high atop a bluff to wait for her cubs, but they never arrived. Mishe Mokwa eventually died and the Great Spirit Manitou made her resting place atop the bluff the Sleeping Bear Dunes. The spirit also raised up two islands, North and South Manitou, to mark the spots where her cubs had died."

"Sad," Claire mused. "But a far more enchanting explanation than receding glaciers and temperature changes."

"You'd rather have fiction than facts?" he asked, glancing sideways as he drove.

"In this case, definitely." She shifted in her seat so she could look at him better. "So, who lives there now?"

"No one," he told her.

If Claire found the legend enchanting, the Manitou Islands' history was no less so. Both islands had once been settled, mainly by European immigrants in the early part of the nineteenth century. Ships had stopped at the islands, where steamers could get wood and food and other supplies were available. In bad weather, captains had charted a course for South Manitou, which provided the only natural harbor along two hundred and twenty miles of Michigan's shore.

"There are several shipwrecks in the area," Ethan told Claire. "The wreck of the *Francisco Morazon,* a

Liberian freighter that got stuck on a sandbar nearly fifty years ago, is visible from the shore."

"It's still there?"

"Uh-huh. It sticks out of the water like a tombstone."

"Creepy." But she laughed.

"Both islands also have abandoned farms, cottages and cemeteries."

"So they're like…ghost towns."

"More or less. Nervous?"

"Never," she assured him.

"There's no place to stop for a latte."

"That's okay. I'm really more of an espresso drinker," she said.

"Ah. Caffeine without all of the frills."

Claire laughed. "Exactly." Then she decided to switch the subject. "You like it up here, obviously. I mean, you built a second home here and you seem to know an awful lot about the area. You must spend a lot of time here."

"I do." His gaze connected with hers for a moment. "Why do I get the feeling that surprises you?"

"I just thought…well, given your job, I figured you probably worked incredibly long hours." She shook her head. "My father practically lives at the office."

"You don't have to be a workaholic to be a success in business, Claire. My schedule doesn't always allow it, but I try to take regular vacations. What's the point in having money if you don't take time to enjoy it?"

"Do you ever get back to Chicago?" she asked.

"No. My family is all in Michigan now. There's nothing in Chicago for me, so I have no reason to go back."

"No reason?" She wasn't sure why his blunt statement bothered her so much, and so she argued, "But you have clients there, according to your Web site."

"I also have people on my payroll to see to those clients' needs," he replied. "I haven't been to Chicago since—" He cleared his throat. "It's been years."

"Maybe you'll come back now." Claire's voice was barely audible over the crunch of gravel under the tires as he pulled into a parking lot.

He'd heard her though. She could tell by the way the muscle in his jaw worked as he switched off the ignition of the SUV. Neither one of them got out.

"Maybe I will," he said at last.

"It's a great city."

"Yes." He studied her for a moment. "I'm beginning to remember."

They walked to the dock. Ethan carried a small backpack with light provisions for their hike to his friend's cottage on the far side of the island. The boat ride out to South Manitou was going to take them an hour and a half. Luckily the weather was good and the water far from choppy.

Still, Claire commented, "Too bad we can't fly. I think your friend should invest in a pilot's license."

"Actually, Oren has one and he owns his own Cessna, but there's no landing strip on the island." Ethan added a heartfelt, "Thank God."

"You still don't like flying," she said.

She recalled how quiet he'd been on their flight to Las Vegas. She'd teased him about it until it had become obvious that his phobia was very real and a source of embarrassment for him. She didn't needle him about it now. Everybody had their own demons to conquer, as she well knew.

"I fly when it's absolutely necessary," he said. "But when I can, I prefer to drive. Besides, you see more that way."

He had a point and so she nodded. "You can see a lot more on a bike too."

Her response had Ethan thinking. "I have to admit, I'm surprised that you ride. And so well. No offense, Claire, but you never struck me as being all that athletic."

"No offense taken. I wasn't athletic."

But she had been slim, Ethan recalled that now. She'd had delicate curves and the softest skin. And though he tried not to, he remembered how she had trembled and gasped the very first time he'd run his callused palms over the subtle flair of her bare hips.

He tried to concentrate on the conversation. Claire was saying, "I never worked out back then beyond taking the stairs at the office if I'd indulged in a really big lunch. I didn't have much in the way of muscle tone."

"So, what turned you on to cycling? Got a thing for men in tight shorts?"

"Who doesn't?" A pair of neatly arched eyebrows bobbed twice for emphasis.

Ethan couldn't help but laugh. "That the only reason?"

"No." She hesitated for a moment, but then shook her head and said dismissively, "It's a long story."

"The boat ride is ninety minutes. Why don't you entertain me?"

"It's not all that entertaining," she replied.

He ran his knuckles down the curve of her cheek. "I'll be the judge."

The chartered boat had an enclosed cabin, but Claire headed to the open bow instead. The wind was stronger now that they were on the water and it carried an added bite. She seemed not to notice. Tilting her head to one side, she studied him for a moment. "Okay, but don't complain if I bore you."

"Wouldn't dream of it. So, should we go inside, get comfortable?" he asked.

Claire shook her head. "Let's stay out here for a few more minutes."

She leaned her elbows on the rail as the boat pushed away from the dock. Her hair was tugged this way and that and her cheeks already glowed red from the cold, but she didn't seem to mind. She looked healthy, fit, confident and too sexy for his peace of mind. Ethan found himself questioning the wisdom of asking her to stay for a couple of days. What exactly was he hoping to gain from renewing their acquaintance? He was usually decisive and clear minded. It bothered him that he didn't have an answer.

"It was a magazine article," she said out of the blue,

raising her voice to be heard over the waves and the engine's throaty hum. "That's what made me buy a bike and start riding in the first place."

"Must have been some article. Did it tout the benefits of cardiovascular fitness or, better yet, claim it was the key to everlasting youth?"

One side of her mouth turned up in a smile. "If it had every woman on the planet would be trading in her night cream for a twenty-one-speed. Actually, it was about a charity that was organizing a four-hundred-kilometer bike trek through the Himalayas."

"I think I saw something about that on the news not long ago."

"It just finished up late last month. It was quite a success. The goal was to raise awareness about and money for street children around the globe. The effort was international, with people from several countries already committed to ride and donations pouring in."

He hadn't expected this. "Yeah. A worthy cause."

"Very."

"So, you just—what?—signed up?" Pretty gutsy, he thought. And he couldn't help but admire the nerve it had taken even though he had firsthand knowledge of Claire's impulsiveness.

But she shook her head. "Not at first. I sent money, a fairly sizable donation, which the Mayfield Corporation generously matched."

"A tax write-off," he said, oddly disappointed.

Claire didn't argue with his assessment. "Uh-huh.

You can never have too many of those, according to both my father and his accountant. But then, a few weeks after I'd mailed the check, I was flicking the television remote one night and I came across a documentary about the lives of street children in some of the world's poorest countries. The conditions, the deprivation, the dangers. I couldn't sleep that night. It really bothered me."

"Our country has those too. Runaways, throwaways. Kids who run wild and loose because their parents are whacked-out on drugs or simply don't give a damn." He gestured with one hand, memories rising despite his best attempts to keep them in check. "Or maybe their parents are there, but, for whatever reason, they're missing in action. Street life can look mighty appealing when there's nothing at home but heartache or chaos."

"Was that what it was like for you?" she asked softly.

He didn't want to talk about this. He'd dealt with it years ago. Yet it bubbled to the surface now. "For a while," he admitted.

"Right after your dad died?"

He gave a jerky nod, intended to say nothing more. The words slipped out though. "My mother was a wreck afterward. He'd left her with nothing but a mountain of debts and three mouths to feed. She had no job, no real marketable job skills, and she ran up more debt trying to keep a roof over our heads, all while suffering from what I realize now was debilitating depression, which she treated by…drinking. After one real bender, a neighbor reported her to the police and the state stepped in and took us away."

"Ethan—"

But he needed to finish now or he knew he wouldn't. Why telling Claire about his not-so-pleasant past was suddenly important, he wasn't sure.

He kept his tone matter-of-fact and continued. "Anyway, we got lucky and all three of us were sent to live with an aunt instead of going to some foster home or different foster homes. My mom got sober and then she took some courses so she could get a better job. She moved into subsidized housing and we got to come home for good a year and a half later."

Claire laid a hand on his arm. "I didn't know how… how difficult you had it growing up."

He shrugged off her sympathy along with her hand and leaned against the rail beside her. His pose was as impassive as his tone. "It's not something I go around talking about."

"Not even to your wife?"

"Maybe if we'd stayed married for more than a couple of days I would have told you."

The reminder of their brief union was intended as a slap. He felt vulnerable and needed to put distance between them. But it was Claire's response that landed a far more powerful blow. "Why did you tell me just now?"

He didn't have an answer for her. It wasn't like him to bare his soul—and to a virtual stranger no less. For all practical purposes, that was what she was, even if she sometimes felt like much more. Even if once, a lifetime ago now, they had held each other through the night and whispered words of love.

"I didn't tell you about it for sympathy, so don't go cueing the violins," he said at last. "I had a good childhood, a generally happy one once my mom got her act together. We just didn't have a lot of money."

"That wasn't an issue for me."

Because he was still feeling exposed, he said in a bored tone, "I suppose you're going to tell me the cliché is true. That money can't buy happiness."

"It *is* true," Claire said with a shrug. She went on. "But no. I had a good childhood. Oh, my dad was overbearing and my mother always complaining about some ailment or another. But I wasn't abused or neg—" Her color deepened with what he suspected was embarrassment.

"Neglected," he supplied.

She cleared her throat. "Yes. Anyway, my parents have always been very generous with me, but it's been on their terms. I didn't mind those terms until I got to be an adult and realized that neither the terms nor my parents had changed, even though I had. They wanted to keep running my life."

The deck rocked gently under their feet, loosening more memories. "As I recall, you didn't put up much of a fight. You let them."

They regarded one another as the boat sliced through the frigid blue water. Up ahead, the island grew closer, its shoreline becoming more distinct. Claire and Ethan were looking back though, churned in the wake of their past.

"You're right. I did let them. But you didn't put up much of a fight either."

"It wasn't my fight to wage, Claire."

"Maybe part of me wanted it to be," she said so quietly that he wasn't sure he'd heard her correctly.

"What? Why?"

She shook her head, looking confused and vulnerable. "It doesn't matter now." She shivered then. "We should go inside. I'm getting cold."

"Me, too." And he was. Chilled to the bone.

Claire felt raw.

Ethan followed her through a metal door to the small cabin. Heat wafted from the vents as they settled on a bench near one of the windows. Neither one of them bothered with the view.

"You're quiet," he observed. "Story time over?"

"If you want it to be."

"You can't just leave me hanging," he drawled. "I've got to know the ending."

His smile was tight, his tone slightly mocking. Claire decided to ignore both and focus on her story.

"That documentary really opened my eyes. Kids barely beyond toddling are out there doing whatever it takes to find food, shelter. They fall prey to all sorts of diseases and maladies, not to mention warped adults." Her face twisted in disgust. "It made me sick and it made me feel…guilty."

His expression grew puzzled. "Why guilty?"

"I've got a lot. Too much, when you get right down to it. And I've never had to work for any of it. It was just handed to me at birth, right along with my family name."

"Yeah. That's a real cross to bear," he muttered sarcastically.

It was as if he was hoping to get a rise out of her. She decided not to let him. Instead, she opted to put him in his place without losing her cool. "Snobbery works both ways, you know."

"Please. I'm not a snob," he objected.

"Let me ask you this. When you have kids some day, are you going to give them the things you wanted to have as a boy but couldn't afford?"

Ethan didn't like the current direction of their conversation any more than he'd liked the previous one. Talking about children with Claire seemed unwise and oddly forbidden. He cleared his throat. "I'm not going to spoil them, but I'm sure as hell not going to deprive them either."

Them. A boy and a girl. Dark hair, inquisitive eyes, freckled noses. The picture of those heretofore faceless, far-in-the-future offspring was much too clear for his comfort.

"I remember you telling me that working for something built character. I believe it was our seventh date."

"A baseball game," he supplied.

She nodded. "The Cubs won, thanks to a three-run homer in the bottom of the seventh."

Ethan blinked. "You didn't strike me as a big fan of the great American pastime," he recalled. "How is it possible that you remember that?"

Claire coughed and her cheeks turned pink. "Every girl remembers her first...baseball game."

Her embarrassment stoked his memory. Then it was his turn to flush. Ethan had made it to "second base" that night and might have had a chance to steal third had her parents not arrived home early from a dinner party. He'd left via the back entrance only because she'd insisted he wasn't in any condition to meet her father. One look down at the front of his jeans and he'd understood perfectly what she'd meant. He shifted uncomfortably on the vinyl seat now as a relapse threatened.

"Forgot about that."

"Thanks." She laughed, but he thought she also looked somewhat insulted.

"Not that it wasn't...memorable. I just haven't dwelled much on that time in my life."

"I haven't either," she said. "But, looking back now, it wasn't all bad, was it?"

"No. Just the ending."

She nodded and knotted her fingers together. "The ending was bad. I never expected it to turn out that way."

"Me, either."

They appeared to be in perfect agreement on the subject. Why did that bother him so much? He cleared his throat. "Getting back to...children, sure, I'm a proponent of making one's own way, but that's not the same as asking a kid to put his paper route money in the household kitty to help buy groceries."

He'd done that as a boy. He was doing his damnedest to make sure if he ever had children they never had to do the same—for their sakes as well as his own. Ethan knew how much it had pained his mother to ask for his weekly earnings.

Claire nodded. "I understand. I'm just saying that parents give their children what they can. Children in affluent families get more because their parents have more to give. It's not necessarily intentional, but sometimes they make things *too* easy for them as a result."

He considered what she'd said and had to concede she had a point. "Okay."

"Well, I wanted to put myself on the line for once. Personally. Giving money is easy enough when you have a lot of it. I wanted to give something else, something that actually *cost* me."

"A noble gesture."

Claire refused the compliment with a shake of her head. "Not really. The article I read quoted several people who had done similar rides for other charitable organizations. They all described the experience as challenging, a journey of self-discovery that only took a matter of weeks to complete but was ultimately life-changing."

"Life-changing?" he repeated skeptically.

Claire sighed. "I know. It sounds like a bunch of psychobabble. My father thought so too. He was all for me giving money to a worthwhile cause, especially if it could get Mayfield some good press. He even suggested that if I wanted to do more I should become a spokesperson for the charity that was sponsoring the ride. But he felt if I needed to *find myself*—his phrase, not mine, by the way—I should look in Chicago rather than remote parts of China."

"I see that your father hasn't changed," Ethan said dryly.

"No. And I was becoming more entrenched too."

"Found yourself in a rut?"

"A rut? No." She shook her head for emphasis. "A hole. An incredibly deep one that I'd dug for myself over the years. I wanted out," she said simply, though he suspected it was not a simple matter, especially when she added, "So I signed up for the ride, bought a bike and started a training regimen."

"When was that?"

"Last spring."

"Get out." He'd expected the answer to be years, not months.

"It's true. Swear." She held up a hand.

"Must have been some training regimen." His gaze meandered over a pair of denim-hugged legs that were crossed at the knee. He'd glimpsed their power when she'd pedaled up the steep hill leading to his house.

"Grueling is the word that comes to mind. I was in so much pain after the first week that I could barely walk. And sitting wasn't much better."

Claire laughed again. He liked the sound, the musical

quality of it. He liked even better the fact that she could laugh at herself. The woman he'd known a decade ago had been far more serious than self-effacing.

"What did your parents think of your ... commitment?"

"They wanted to *have* me committed." But she wasn't laughing now. She was hardly smiling. "They thought I was crazy. I'm pretty sure they still do, especially now that I've moved into the city and quit the company."

"You've been busy. But they had to have been proud of you. I'm proud." He poked her in the ribs and, to keep the moment light, added, "And I barely like you, remember?"

She smiled, but it didn't reach her eyes. "I think for a while there my dad was a little impressed by the kind of dedication I was showing. He commented on it a couple of times even. But now that the trip is over they are not quite so enamored with its, um, life-changing properties," she said dryly.

"Change can be…unsettling. Especially when you don't see it coming," he added in a hoarse whisper.

Wasn't that the truth? Ethan had thought he'd known what he was letting himself in for when he'd invited Claire along today. Now, he wasn't so sure.

The woman was full of surprises. He didn't like surprises. He hated them, in fact, since she'd sprung a couple of doozies on him in the past. Still, he found himself wondering—eagerly anticipating, even—what discovery he would make next.

"We've arrived," Claire said.

She stood after the boat bumped gently against the dock.

"No. We still have a way to go," he replied.

She turned, her expression puzzled.

"Oren's cottage. It's quite a hike," he explained.

But Ethan wasn't at all sure that was what he had meant.

CHAPTER SEVEN

ETHAN AND CLAIRE started their hike just beyond the lighthouse to the south of the dock. Oren's cottage was on the other side of the island, not far inland from the Perched Sand Dunes that lined the western coast. They could cut through the middle of the island, where the terrain would be more rugged. Instead, he suggested they follow a hiking trail that hugged the shoreline for part of the way.

"The scenery is spectacular, even this time of the year, but only if you think you're up to it," he said again. She definitely saw a smile this time.

"You know that I am. Cycling four hundred kilometers, remember?"

"I remember that, what I don't recall is you being this competitive."

"It's a newly acquired trait." Sending him a sideways smile, she asked, "Do you like it?"

"Does my opinion matter to you?"

"Not in the least." She laughed then, appearing to enjoy his surprise at her bluntness.

"So, you're done living your life for others?" Ethan asked. Claire had said so before, but for some reason he wanted to hear her say it again.

"I am." Her smile turned cocky then as she pressed ahead of him. "Come on, Seaver. You're falling behind. Getting winded already?"

"Hardly." He accelerated his pace to match hers.

After a few minutes of power walking, Ethan slowed. "Why don't we call this a draw?"

Claire shrugged. She wasn't even winded, he realized, when she said, "If you say so."

He laughed and then bent to pick up a flat stone, which he threw. It skipped twice over the surface of the water before finally sinking. Claire picked up a rock and tossed it too. Hers, however, sank immediately.

She faced him, frowning. "How did you do that?"

"It's all in the wrist."

"Do it again."

He obliged her. This time the stone skipped three times before submerging. Claire's second effort, however, garnered the same results as her first. She muttered something. Yes, she was definitely much more competitive these days.

"Your angle's off," Ethan told her. "You can't just lob it out there like a baseball. You have to aim at the horizon." He came up beside her and reached for her arm, gently propelling it forward and back. "Like this. It's more of a sideways motion, like you're tossing a Frisbee. See?"

"Sideways motion. Got it." The wind lifted the ends of her hair, which tickled his cheek, and he caught a faint whiff of her perfume. He remembered that scent. He remembered watching her dab it behind her ears, on the insides of her wrists, between her breasts. Claire turned her head and smiled. Ethan coughed and stepped back.

"Go ahead. Give it a try."

She tossed the stone, this time following his advice. One, two, three times it bounced off the water before going under.

"Did you see that? I did it! I did it!" She twirled in a circle and pumped her fists in the air, looking ridiculously pleased with herself. Looking just a little too lovely for his peace of mind.

And so he said teasingly, "That was just beginner's luck."

Giving him a pointed look, she picked up another stone and tossed it. It didn't go as far as the first, but she eked out two small skips. Afterward she settled her hands on her hips. "What do you say now?"

Ethan shrugged. "You always were a fast learner."

"You always were a good teacher."

She glanced away after saying it, looking slightly embarrassed, leaving him to wonder if she was also remembering the night they'd first made love. He'd been the teacher then too, and she an eager, apt pupil.

"We'd better get going," he said quickly.

Claire stuffed her hands into the pockets of the down vest and nodded. They walked nearly a mile and at a pace brisk enough to keep conversation at a minimum and them both from complaining about the sharp bite of the wind.

"So, what are you going to do with your life now that you're unemployed?" he asked.

"I've been thinking about that." She slowed to kick a small piece of driftwood across the sand. "To tell you the truth, I'm not sure."

"There's no rush. In fact, it's not like you need to work at all," he pointed out.

"That's true enough. If I don't pull in a paycheck, I won't starve or become homeless or anything. But I also won't be very happy, so I guess it depends on your definition of need."

"I'd be curious to hear yours."

She stopped walking and watched him carefully for a moment. Finally, she said, "I need to feel part of something bigger than myself. I want to leave my mark somehow."

Ethan was a bit surprised, but pleasantly so. He liked her answer. "Have you thought about philanthropy?" he asked.

"Do you mean like setting up a foundation or something?"

"Yes. In addition to money, you've already got a lot of the right connections. You could do a lot of good."

She started walking again. "I hadn't considered that, but you're right. There's always a need."

He nodded. "When I was a kid, there were some nice people who helped out my family when my mom fell apart, but government assistance only goes so far, you know. Sometimes it takes private dollars to fill in the gaps. I'd like to do something similar in the future. Unfortunately, I'm not in a position to do that at this point."

She smiled. "Thank you."

"For what?"

"For being one of the few people who take me seriously."

"Claire…" He swallowed, not sure what to say. Then he held out a hand. "Come on, there's something I want to show you."

Claire thought Ethan meant the shipwreck that was visible from the shore, but with only a glance at the rusting, wave-battered hull, he headed away from the beach.

"This way."

"What do you want to show me?" she asked. She was curious about that, but even more curious about the warmth spreading up her arm from the hand he was holding.

"You'll see," he said.

After a few minutes of walking she did.

"Oh, my God." The words slipped out in a reverent whisper and for one crazy moment she had an almost overpowering urge to genuflect. They were surrounded by a stand of massive, towering conifers.

Ethan nodded and grinned. "That was my reaction the first time I came upon them too."

"What kind of trees are these?" She tipped her head back as she let out a long, low whistle that seemed to echo off the fragrant boughs that blotted out the midday sky.

"They're white cedar." He was still holding her hand. He released it now to make a sweeping gesture. "They call this the Valley of the Giants."

"I can see why." She walked to the base of one of the monsters and leaned against its trunk. "How old do you think this tree is?"

He hunched his shoulders. "I'm no expert, but I've read that some of them are estimated to be more than five hundred years old."

She whistled again and ran her gloved hands over the rough, grayish bark in awe. "Just imagine all of the history they've witnessed and all of the changes they've seen."

"You're not going to hug that tree, are you?"

She scowled at him over one shoulder. "I might."

"I never would have taken you for the outdoors type, Claire." Just as he had earlier when he'd asked her about cycling, he sounded surprised now too.

Claire turned. "That's because I wasn't. Until recently, the closest I ever came to camping was staying in a hotel that didn't offer turndown service."

"Well, that's roughing it," Ethan said dryly. "No chocolate on the pillow? That's positively primitive."

"Smart aleck." But Claire chuckled and admitted, "Believe me, it seemed that way at the time. It all comes down to one's frame of reference, you know."

"So, to what do you attribute this newfound love of the great outdoors?"

"I wouldn't necessarily call it love." She pursed her lips, thinking of the spider that had wiggled its way into her backpack in China and sent her into a shrieking fit that had echoed through the mountain range. "More like appreciation, maybe even respect. I guess you could say the journey through the Himalayas broadened my horizons and introduced me to a lot of new things."

"It seems to keep coming back to that trip," he murmured. "It sounds as if it was a real defining moment for you."

"It was." She moistened her lips. "It's the reason I'm here with you at this very moment, Ethan."

"You've changed." He cleared his throat. "I mean, that's what you've told me a couple of times now."

She tipped her head to one side. "Are you starting to believe me yet?"

"You aren't the same," he agreed quietly, but the groove that appeared between his eyebrows left her to wonder if he was convinced that was a good thing.

"I learned a lot of things about myself on that ride."

"Such as?" He stepped closer, crowding her space. She felt trapped between firm muscle and hard wood. It wasn't the bark that made her fingers itch.

Since the conversation had turned too serious, she decided to keep it light. "Well, for starters, I can fall asleep just about anywhere. We sometimes had to pitch tents or make do with pretty primitive lodgings."

Ethan's gaze lowered in slow increments. "Sorry, but I'm having a hard time picturing you in a sleeping bag."

One dark eyebrow shot up, taking her pulse with it. "On satin sheets, sure."

"Satin." God help her, the word came out on a sigh.

"Yes. But wrapped up in flannel?" He shook his head.

Under his assessing gaze, her body tightened, tingled, proving to be an appalling traitor. "A-actually, I prefer cotton. Six hundred thread count Egyptian cotton, to be precise."

"Your preference is so noted."

Ethan stepped away then and pulled the small pack off his shoulder. He fished out a bottle of water and, after twisting off the cap, he handed it to her. Claire drank deeply. Her throat felt parched. When she handed it back, he took a long swig too. She stared at his mouth. It was wide and sexy...and he knew how to use it.

When she continued to gaze at his lips, lost in memories that were as stubbornly rooted as the giant cedars, Ethan said, "Don't keep me in suspense, Claire."

"Wh-what?"

"I'm dying to hear the rest of your story."

Unfortunately, her mind remained damningly blank, forcing her to ask, "Where was I?"

"In a tent," he supplied. Those sexy lips twitched. "Zipped into flannel."

"Oh, right." Thankfully, another memory came to mind then, this one far more comical than carnal. Her shoulders began to shake with mirth.

"Private joke or are you going to share?"

"I was just recalling the first time my friends and I had to pitch a tent all by ourselves." She gave him a brief physical description of the bombshell Belle and the svelte Simone. "None of us was particularly adept at that kind of thing. It took us more than two hours and halfway through the night the thing toppled over on us."

"What did you do?"

"The only thing we could under the circumstances. We rolled over and went back to sleep. We were too damned sore and exhausted to care." She patted the thick tree trunk. "Thank you for bringing me here, Ethan."

"Well, you did say you needed to be part of something bigger than yourself."

"Yes I did." Claire's laughter echoed through the forest.

"From the sound of things, I'd say that bike trip qualifies too." His expression sobered. "I'm proud of you, Claire."

"Thank you." Her lips bowed with a smile. "For the first time in my life, I'm proud of me, too." When the silence stretched into something awkward, she decided to change the subject. "I wish I had my camera. These trees are incredible, inspiring…amazing."

"You might want to save some of those adjectives."

"Why?"

"You haven't seen the dunes yet. Come on." Once again, he held out his hand. When Claire slipped hers into it this time, she tried not to question the rightness she felt.

Ethan was right. The dunes were a sight to behold.

They angled down to the water like a vast carpet of gold, shot through with the greenish-brown threads of grass.

"Come on," she coaxed as they stood at the top and looked out over the great lake. "Let's run down to the water."

"I don't think that's a good idea."

"It's not that far."

"Down," he agreed. "The way back up will seem like a turn in purgatory."

"You're probably right." But then she grinned devilishly. "I'll race you."

She was off like a shot, turning to send him an overly confident salute just before losing her footing. It was all a blur after that as she tumbled head over heels through sand and errant clumps of sharp-bladed grass the rest of the way to the bottom.

"Claire!" Ethan hollered. He swore his heart stopped at the sight of her lying on the sand near the shore. He shucked off the backpack and started down after her, sacrificing pride and his own precarious balance in his haste. Even before he managed to stop somersaulting, he heard her throaty laughter.

"What a rush!" she exclaimed, sounding oddly satisfied.

"I take it you're okay," he muttered. For his part it was hard to tell which had taken the most abuse—his head and shoulders or his tailbone.

"Fine, well, besides feeling like an idiot." She chuckled again and stood to shake the sand from her clothes.

"It was a stupid thing to do," he admonished. He stayed where he was, still not certain he was ready to move.

"Well, it's not like it was intentional. The fall, I mean."

She shrugged off his rebuke and smiled, appearing radiant and relaxed. Her cheeks glowed rosy and her eyes were bright with an irresistible combination of mischief and merriment.

"Come on, admit it. Once you realized you hadn't died, that was pretty incredible."

He glanced away and muttered, "You took ten years off my life."

Her good humor remained, though. "Actually, I think it was your own fall that did that. Thanks for coming to my rescue, by the way."

He snorted. "Carry me back up to the top and we'll call it even."

"Sorry. I guess I'll have to remain in your debt." But she walked to where he still lay prone in the sand and offered him her hand. "Come on."

Ethan accepted her hand, but only so he could pull her down. She landed on top of him, sprawled half across his chest. Awareness took the place of amusement.

"Wh-what are you doing?" she asked.

"Haven't got a clue." It was a hell of an admission for a man who'd spent years strategically mapping out his every move both professionally and personally. "Maybe it was a mistake to bring you here today. Maybe it was a mistake to ask you to stay in Glen Arbor in the first place."

"Why?"

"It was a whole lot easier to hate you, Claire."

He raised his head off the sand and kissed her, starting out slow to give her the opportunity to pull away and end it. She didn't. Instead, she leaned in, changing the set of their mouths and accelerating the tempo. Ethan's response was instantaneous and urgent. His arms tightened around her and he rolled until he was the one on top.

"I want you," he murmured against her lips. "It's a fact I can't change."

"But you want to change it."

He said nothing. Even so, Claire replied, "I know. The feeling's mutual."

He rolled off her and rose to his feet. She accepted the hand he offered to help her up.

Their climb to the top of the dune was pure hell on the quadriceps. Claire was going to be pathetically sore come the morning. Of course, she had no one to blame but herself. Just as she had no one to blame but herself that her lingering attraction to Ethan was threatening to transform into something far more consuming.

Oren Delacroix's cottage was a quaint bungalow that had been built in 1932. It was bounded by woods on three sides, with its front opening onto a meadow. Brown grass and the dried stalks of wild flowers rustled in the November breeze.

Their host came out onto the porch just as they turned up the flagstone walk.

"You made it," Oren called. He was about half a head

shorter than Ethan and wider in girth. "I was getting a little worried. I called the boat captain and he said he'd dropped you off a few hours ago."

"We took the long way," Ethan said. "This is Claire."

"Hello, Claire. And welcome. Ethan mentioned he was bringing a guest. I figured it was James. You're better looking, by the way."

Claire laughed, but the lingering awkwardness between her and Ethan made it sound forced. "It's nice to meet you." She walked up the steps, holding out a hand, which Oren shook.

Ethan joined them on the porch. "James says hello."

"Is he in Glen Arbor, then?"

"Yes, but he'd rather spend all of his time with his wife."

"That's love for you. Makes it impossible to stay apart." Oren divided an assessing look between the pair of them. Claire felt her face heat. It was a relief when the man said, "Well, come inside and get warm. I've got hot chocolate made and dinner in the oven."

"You cooked?" Ethan looked queasy.

"I can warm up a catered feast with the best of them, my friend."

The interior of the house was as quaint and lovely as the view from its porch. It was small, barely more than a thousand square feet, but cozy rather than cramped. They settled around a vintage chrome-legged table in the kitchen.

"So, how do you know Ethan?" Oren asked.

Claire wrapped her hands around the mug of hot chocolate. "We um, we—"

"Go back a ways," Ethan finished for her.

"Ethan and I go back a ways too," Oren said.

"He mentioned that you helped him get his business going when he was first starting out," Claire said.

Oren nodded. "I wish I could take credit for Seaver becoming a success, but the truth is other than providing him with a few leads at the beginning, he did it all by himself. And now he's poised to expand."

Even though her father had told her as much, Claire said, "Really?"

"I'm sure Claire's not interested in talking business." Ethan shifted in his seat.

"I don't mind."

Oren continued, "Seaver is doing very well in the Midwest. Ethan is the go-to guy for every sizable company or corporation when it comes to providing customized security systems and technical support. Now he's interested in developing new technologies. He even holds a patent on an alarm system."

"Terrific." She glanced at Ethan, impressed.

"Of course to do more in that area takes serious capital," Oren was saying.

"Any leads?" Claire asked Ethan.

"Nothing I can talk about at the moment."

"Well, I'm sure it will all work out."

It was dark when they returned to Glen Arbor. The moon was out and nearly full, illuminating the leaf-scattered walk that led to the bed-and-breakfast. The porch light was on and a lamp glowed softly from inside.

Claire pulled the key from her purse when they reached the door and then turned. It came as a shock to realize she was nervous. Would he kiss her again? She recalled the way he'd held her on the dunes, his frame pressing into hers. God help her, she hadn't wanted Ethan to stop. A relationship didn't fit into her current plans, especially a relationship with this man. No matter how many times she told herself that, though, her body just wouldn't cooperate.

So she sounded a little breathless when she said, "Thank you for today. I had a nice time."

"Me, too. Will you be leaving tomorrow?" he asked.

"Assuming I can get a flight, yes."

"I guess this is goodbye then."

"I guess so," she said.

Neither one of them moved. The wind kicked up, groaning eerily through the bare trees and sending dead leaves swirling.

"This is awkward," Ethan said at last.

Claire laughed. "Very."

"I feel like there's something more I should say, but I can't think of what it might be, you know?"

"Exactly."

"I don't think I need to tell you I wasn't happy to see you when you first arrived, but I am glad you stayed. I'm glad we had a chance to talk, to settle things." He reached out to give her elbow a squeeze through the quilted sleeve of her jacket.

And even though things felt further than ever from settled, she said, "I'm glad too."

CHAPTER EIGHT

CLAIRE AWOKE AT twenty past eight. Sleep had been fitful and her dreams an odd blend of past and present. She stretched on the room's antique four-poster bed and felt her muscles protest. She was sore, just as she'd figured she would be from that trek up the dunes. But there was another ache that bothered her even more. She was leaving today and she wanted to stay.

Claire also wanted to stand on her own and exercise this independence that was so new to her. Her desires seemed at odds with one another. But there was no denying the chemistry that existed between her and Ethan.

She tried to approach the matter analytically.

How practical was it to try to develop, let alone sustain, any kind of relationship when they lived several hours apart? Of course, Belle and Simone lived several time zones away and she didn't regard that as an impediment to their staying in touch, not with the Internet, telephone and text messaging. But with Ethan it was... different. She wanted close, physical contact.

She rolled over, buried her face in the pillow and groaned. So much for being analytical. Maybe her friends could offer some insight into the matter. Claire tossed back the covers, went to her computer and booted it up.

The first thing she saw when she connected to the Internet was Simone's message. It was on the top of her mailbox. Claire would have opened it first anyway, but the Read This Immediately subject line sealed the deal. She double-clicked on the e-mail and held her breath, only to have it sputtering out a moment later along with the words "Thank you, God!"

The reporter wasn't going to go public with their secrets. Simone trusted his word that the contents of her diary would not be published in any way, shape or form.

Claire wrote back, copying her reply to Belle:

You must be thrilled! I know I am. Makes me want to take back every last nasty thought I had about Ryan Tanner. Apparently the man has a conscience after all. If you have reason to speak to him again, you may pass along my appreciation that he exercised good judgment on this matter.

She tapped an index finger against her lips and considered how to word the rest of the letter:

I'm still in Glen Arbor, but planning to return home later today. Something here still seems, well, unresolved. It has nothing to do with the past. I think Ethan and I have reached an understanding on that score. It seems we had both made assumptions that turned out to be wrong.

She gave them a brief summary of events regarding the uncashed check and its subsequent return.

No, it's not the past that's troubling me. It's the future.
You asked me before, Belle, what my feelings for Ethan were. In China, even in Chicago, I thought I knew. Now I'm very confused. I don't really want to be in a relationship right now, assuming Ethan is interested in one, and I think he is. But I can't deny the attraction I feel and it's mutual. So, if either of you has any good advice to share, I'd love to hear it.

She hit Send and was gratified when, a moment later, she received a reply. It was from Simone:

We don't get to choose the timing of our relation-ships, Claire. Nor do we get to choose to whom we are attracted. I'm discovering that myself. You married him once. Maybe there was more to it than what you've long thought.

Claire nibbled her lip. Maybe.
Then she smiled as she read the rest of Simone's message. It was the mention of Ryan Tanner's name that had Claire wondering if she wasn't the only one with man trouble.

Claire logged off and stowed her computer. Her mind was made up. She would catch a late flight to Chicago. Before then she needed to see Ethan. She had news to share. Good news for a change. It warranted a personal visit, rather than a mere phone call, she rationalized. There was nothing rational, however, about the way she fussed with her appearance for the next hour.

Ethan woke to the scent of coffee and the low murmur of conversation coming from downstairs. He glanced at the clock. It was nearly ten. He rarely slept so late, but then he hadn't managed to drift off until after two a.m.

Claire.

The woman had a habit of disturbing his peace. Good thing she would soon be back in Chicago. He scrubbed a hand down his face. Yeah, good thing. Right.

The way he felt at the moment told Ethan it didn't matter whether they were separated by a few miles of town or hundreds of miles of lake, he would be thinking about her. She'd done that to him in the past, too. Tied him in knots. He was older now, wiser. Unfortunately, he didn't appear to have any more control over his emotions.

He glanced at the telephone on his bedside table. He could call her. And say what? Stay another day? To what end? A dead end, his more practical side said. He picked up the phone and dialed anyway.

"She's not here," the bed-and-breakfast owner told him when she came on the line a moment later.

"I see. Thank you." He hung up.

Well, that settled it, he told himself as he stared at the ceiling. Claire had left town already. Good. Good riddance. The chapter could be closed.

He grabbed a quick shower, pulled on a pair of jeans and a sweater and then stumbled to the kitchen with his hair still wet. Coffee. He needed caffeine. Laura and James were seated at the table, their hands touching, their gazes locked. He wanted to be disgusted by the syrupy display of affection. He found himself envious instead.

He grabbed the coffeepot. Half a cup remained in the bottom of the carafe.

"I guess it's too much to expect you lovebirds to leave some java for the host," he muttered.

"Sorry about that. I meant to make another pot, but we got talking about baby names. I'll make it now." Laura blushed and rose awkwardly from her seat, making him feel small.

"Someone got up on the wrong side of the bed," James said.

"Sorry. You're right. I'll make the coffee," Ethan told Laura. But she was already filling the top of the maker with fresh water.

"I don't mind." Then her gaze strayed to the window over the sink. "Someone's here, Ethan."

Ethan stepped over and peered outside. He recognized the driver instantly.

"Claire." The name came out on a smile.

"Isn't that the woman from the grill?" Laura said.

He cleared his throat. "Yes."

"You didn't seem sure if you knew her or not," his brother said.

"I know her."

"Well, you might have told us you were expecting company for breakfast," Laura admonished. "I would have dressed."

"I wasn't expecting her." Hoping he'd see her again was something else entirely.

"Well, she's here now. You have to invite her in," Laura said.

He made a sound that was not quite a yes and not quite a no. The last thing he wanted at the moment was to subject Claire to his family's scrutiny. No. That wasn't quite true. He didn't want to subject himself to it. He had little doubt they would figure out soon enough that the Claire on the doorstep was the Claire he'd been married to long ago.

Although he hadn't shared many particulars about their brief relationship with his brothers, they knew he'd recklessly flown to Vegas, taken vows and then returned home without a bride, *sans* a job and surly beyond measure. Not long after that he'd moved to Detroit. Determined to keep her brood together, his mother had moved to Michigan, too. James had still been in high school, so he'd come with her. Michael, who'd been in college, had relocated after graduation.

James joined them at the window, nudging Ethan to the side so he could get a better look as Claire opened the car door and got out. "Hmm. She's got a classy look about her."

"Sophisticated," Laura offered. "Even wearing blue jeans. I'm thinking designer label and pricey." She made a humming noise. "And so put together with that tweed jacket, those boots. She looks like a fashion model, except she's too petite."

They both turned and looked expectantly at Ethan.

"What?"

"Who is she? What does she do? Where does she live? And how long have you been dating?" Laura covered all of the bases in a single breath.

He answered the question that made him the most nervous first.

"We're not dating." The words came out a little too fast. The rest of his explanation was tortuously slow and disjointed. "We're…we're… Claire and I are… That is, we're…"

Just what in the hell were they? And why couldn't he think of a single word to sum up their relationship now when dozens of them had come readily to mind in the past?

Claire was walking toward the house. "Could we please move away from the window?" Ethan pleaded.

After running a hand through his hair, Ethan went to open the door.

"Good morning," Claire said.

"Good morning. I thought you'd left. I called the bed-and-breakfast and they said you were gone."

"You called?"

He cleared his throat. "I was wondering what time your flight was."

"I haven't scheduled one yet. I wanted to see you. I probably should have called first." She motioned toward his hair. "Did you just get out of the shower?"

"A few minutes ago. I slept late." And poorly.

"Aren't you going to invite your guest in?" his sister-in-law called. "It's awfully cold out there this morning to conduct a conversation on the doorstep."

Despite the freezing temperature Ethan felt his face heat and he grimaced. "That's Laura," he told Claire. "She and James are in the kitchen."

Claire's expression mirrored his chagrin. "I forgot you had company."

So had he. Ethan stepped back to allow her inside. She hadn't even cleared the threshold when James joined Ethan in the entryway. "We're not company. We're family," he said with a broad smile. He held out a hand. "Claire, is it? I'm James. My brother has told us absolutely nothing about you. Why don't you stay for breakfast? My wife is going to make pancakes."

Ethan had little doubt that in short order Claire would be divested of her coat and gloves and ushered to the kitchen, where the grilling would begin in earnest.

"Actually, I think Claire and I will go out to eat."

"Oh, Ethan, no," she sputtered, dividing a horrified look between the brothers. "I…I can come back later or you can meet me in town after you've had breakfast."

His mind was made up, though. He was already

slipping on shoes and reaching into the foyer closet for his coat. Tugging it on, he said, "Come on."

Claire sent an apology in his brother's direction as Ethan pulled her out the door behind him.

He let her drive since he didn't have his car keys with him. Come to that, he didn't have his wallet.

"You're buying, by the way," he informed her as she turned the vehicle around in the amply proportioned driveway and started back down the hill.

"I guess that's the least I can do. I didn't mean to take you away from a meal with your family."

"My sister-in-law does make excellent pancakes," he replied. "And I have maple syrup, the real thing. I bought it at a roadside stand. The Amish make it. It was tapped from local trees last spring. I was really looking forward to tasting it." His gaze cut to her lips, lingered there. "I've had it before. It's incredibly sweet. Impossible to forget."

"Sorry. I should have called. I wasn't thinking."

Ethan chuckled, his previous foul mood forgotten. "For once, Claire, I find myself grateful for your impulsiveness.

She glanced sideways at him. "Why is that?"

"I woke up thinking about you this morning," he surprised them both by admitting.

"What a coincidence." Her lips curved.

Ethan's pulse quickened. "Is that what brought you to my house?"

"Yes." The whispered word was followed quickly by a vehement, "No!" Then Claire hit the brakes, skidding on the gravel before finally coming to a stop.

"Jeez! No need to put me through the windshield just because you can't make up your mind."

"Sorry. It's not that." She laughed, banged her palms on the steering wheel. "I can't believe I forgot the real reason for my visit. I received an e-mail from my friend Simone in Australia. Everything's okay. Nothing's going to be published."

"That's…terrific," he said, trying to make the mental shift from sex to business.

"Yes, it is." She leaned back in her seat, turned her head on the padded rest and smiled at him. "I'm so relieved."

Ethan forced himself to focus on their conversation rather than the way the morning light was teasing burnished highlights from her dark hair. "Are you sure this guy really means it? After all, reporters generally aren't known for their willingness to let go of a story, especially one as potentially sensational as this one."

"I know, but Simone says Ryan Tanner has given her his word."

"His word." Ethan nodded. "And she trusts him to keep it?"

"I believe so. Yes."

"That's good."

"Very."

"Trust is mighty important," he said slowly.

"It's the foundation for any solid relationship." She straightened in her seat.

"Exactly. I mean, if two people can't trust one another, then nothing else really matters." He could see her eyes clearly thanks to her new hairstyle. Even so, he reached out to tuck the short ends of her hair behind one ear. He needed to touch her.

"You have to have trust," she agreed. Her gaze remained steady on his, oddly intense. "And it's something that must be earned."

"Especially once it's been breached."

"Yes, especially then." She moistened her lips. "Of course, re-establishing trust takes time."

"And effort." Ethan leaned closer.

"Uh-huh. Hard work." She leaned in as well.

"Diligence," he murmured, as their lips met briefly.

"You've got to want it." Her breath was hot against his cheek.

Want it? Oh, yes, he wanted it all right, he thought as Claire's lips brushed against his mouth again and hormones jolted through him like a lightning strike. Then her hands came up to frame his face. He strained to get closer, but he couldn't manage it with a seat belt holding him back. She apparently reached the same conclusion. They unbuckled simultaneously and reached for one another once more, this time having to contend with the gear shift and console in their quest to bridge the gap between their bodies.

Obstacles. There always seemed to be too damned many of them.

"This is crazy." Ethan released Claire and slumped back in his seat, his head on the rest, eyes pinched closed as he willed his body to loosen, relax.

"I know."

Beside him, he heard Claire exhale slowly. It didn't help to realize she was as wound up as he felt, even if it was a boost to his ego.

"But, then, maybe sanity is overrated," she added quietly.

He turned his head and opened his eyes so that he could study her. What exactly was she saying? And why was it he wanted to agree with her?

"I'd forgotten how it could be." Her voice was a husky whisper.

"What do you mean?"

"This. What happens between us." She touched her lips, exhaled again. "Over the years I'd forgotten."

Ethan hadn't, even though he'd done his damnedest to convince himself that he had. But the truth was that memories of Claire and his outrageous reaction to her had lurked in his subconscious. She'd been the woman he'd measured all others against, waiting for this same sweet, insatiable heat to flare and consume him.

"It was a long time ago," he said, not sure who he was trying to convince.

"And we're different people."

Yes, but she'd felt the same in his arms: perfect. Ethan coughed. "We're older now."

"Wiser."

His gaze dipped to her lips. "Better?"

"Seemed that way to me," she murmured.

He didn't want to know, he certainly had no business

asking, but he did so anyway, curiosity demanding to be satisfied since his body was being denied. "Have you had much…practice?"

Her cheeks flushed, but her gaze never wavered. "That's an interesting question. Why don't you answer it first?"

He grimaced. "Consider it withdrawn."

"Ah, yes." She chuckled. "Definitely wiser."

Her right hand was resting on the console. Ethan picked it up, stroked the back of it with his thumb. "What are we doing, Claire? We can't go back."

"No, and I don't want to. But we can travel forward. Together. And try to figure out where the road we're on right now leads."

"What if it leads nowhere?" he asked. "What if we still wind up alone and moving in different directions?"

She was quiet for a long moment. Finally, she replied, "Well, I guess at least then we'd know for sure. So, the better question is, do you want to find out?"

He brought the hand he'd been holding to his lips and kissed the back of it. "I do."

Ethan didn't miss the irony that the last time he'd said those particular words to a woman—*this woman*—he'd wound up bitter, broken and alone.

CHAPTER NINE

CLAIRE BOUGHT BREAKFAST, which made it only fair that Ethan offer to buy her dinner that night. Neither of them mentioned that in order for that to happen, she would be postponing her return to Chicago once again.

"You were a cheap date for breakfast," she teased as they drove back to his house. "I don't plan to be a cheap date for dinner. I'm going to order surf and turf and the best bottle of wine the restaurant has in its cellar."

"Not champagne?"

"It will depend on if I feel like celebrating." She sent him a wink.

"What about dessert?" he asked.

"Oh, definitely, and coffee to wash it down."

"You sure eat a lot," he replied. "Good thing you work out or you'd be a little on the chubby side."

She chuckled and found the courage to say, "I wonder how our date will end?"

"How do you want it to end?" The tone of his voice had changed from teasing to a husky whisper.

Claire moistened her lips. "Maybe with a walk in the moonlight. We could hold hands, gaze up at the stars."

"And make a wish?"

She flashed him a grin, even as her heart bumped around in her chest. "Why not?"

"What will you wish for, Claire?"

You. The answer seemed to echo in her head, getting louder and more insistent to be given voice. But she said, "If I tell you, it won't come true."

"Old wives' tale," Ethan countered.

"You go first, then. What would you wish for?"

"Oh, I have something in mind," he evaded with a grin. "So after we do our wishing, what then?"

His smile made her bold. "You'll kiss me."

"In the moonlight?"

She nodded. "Under the stars."

"Will I still be holding your hand?"

"If you want to be."

"And if I want more than that, Claire? What if holding your hand isn't enough?"

Her body tingled head to toe, but she rolled her eyes and forced a smile to her lips. "Men and sex."

To Claire it sounded as if he said, "It goes beyond sex."

They were both quiet for the rest of the ride to his house.

"Well, thanks for the meal," Ethan said after she'd shifted the car into Park. He gave Claire a peck on the cheek, got out and came around to the driver's side door, where he motioned for her to roll down her window. Where the kiss had been chaste, his gaze burned with passion.

"I'll pick you up at six," he told her.

"I'll be waiting."

Claire spent the late afternoon scouring the boutiques in and around Glen Arbor, looking for something spectacular to wear on her date with Ethan.

Date. With Ethan.

The mere words had her smiling as she thumbed through a rack of dresses. She and Ethan had gone out plenty of times before their marriage, of course, but it had never been like this. Nor had she ever felt like this. Or, if she had, she'd chalked up the quaking in her belly to a guilty conscience and a virgin's curiosity.

Well, no guilty conscience or curiosity this time. The only thing she felt, in addition to a delicious amount of anticipation, was a dollop of apprehension. After all, it had been a long time, a *really* long time, since she and Ethan had made love.

With two hours to go before he was due to arrive, she filled up the old-fashioned claw-foot tub in her room's attached bathroom and lowered herself into its jasmine-scented water for a good, long soak. Forty minutes later, freshly shaved, exfoliated and moisturized, she applied her makeup, using a bit more on her eyes than she usually did. Then she set to work on her hair.

She was getting better at styling it. She'd had it cut just before leaving for China. In the Himalayas, she'd let it dry naturally, applying no gel or mousse or spray. Why bother, when a helmet would be strapped on her head all day? Since returning, however, she'd tried to tame its natural waves into a trendy style with a round brush and blow dryer as her stylist had suggested. Now, she smiled at her reflection in the bathroom mirror, satisfied with her efforts.

In the bedroom, she checked the clock and then slipped into the lacy black unmentionables she'd laid out on the bed. She hadn't been able to get an appointment for a manicure and pedicure at a local salon, so she painted her nails herself, choosing a shade of red aptly called Fiery Passion.

Finally she dressed, grabbed the new full-length wool coat and clutch purse she'd purchased for the evening, and headed downstairs.

"Don't you look nice," June said when Claire entered the bed-and-breakfast's front parlor just before Ethan was due to arrive.

"Thank you. The dress is new," she confessed with a grin. "I bought it this afternoon at that little boutique just off the main road."

"I know the one. They have some great finds in there, although I suspect you'd look like a million bucks even if you were decked out in burlap."

"Thanks." Claire appreciated the compliment. She'd never been curvy or well endowed and so she'd generally steered clear of tight-fitting or revealing clothes. Tonight, however, she'd broken with tradition and was pleased with the results. Maybe it was her new toned physique. Maybe it was her new sense of adventure. Whatever the reason, she'd selected something far more daring.

The dress was black, which was its only bow to conservatism since the cut screamed *va-va-va-voom!* Its skirt wasn't overly short, but it followed closely the line of her legs to just above her knees, a slit up the back the only reason she could walk without hobbling. The top dipped low both in the front and the back, its tight sleeves ending midway to her wrists. It wasn't sleazy, but it certainly had the sexy label all sewn up.

The shoes she'd chosen to go with it added a few inches to her diminutive height and highlighted her calves and firm derrière. She was proud of her legs and butt and was only too happy to show them off. No liposuction or implants or anything artificial had been involved in getting them. Just plain old sweat and a lot of pedal pumping.

The doorbell chimed and Claire's nerves churned, turning her confidence shaky. Suddenly she felt conspicuous, like Cinderella, only in reverse. Questions bubbled, doubts beckoned. What if Ethan was wearing a simple pair of blue jeans and his leather jacket, or something else that was relatively casual? Here she was, decked out to the nines. It was obvious that she had primped. It was obvious that she had toiled over her appearance, hoping to impress him. Even as she wondered if he would be pleased with the results, she worried that he would think her shallow and self-absorbed…like he believed she had been.

"I'll get it," June said, giving Claire's arm a reassuring squeeze. "I hope you don't mind, but I want to witness your man's expression when he sees you."

Your man. Was that what he was?

Claire smiled her thanks, even as she considered turning tail and running up the stairs to her room.

"Ready?" June asked.

No. Not even close. But she took a deep breath, exhaled slowly, willed her lips to curve and nodded.

Ethan smiled at the woman who opened the door. Then he looked past her and felt his lungs constrict. There stood Claire, somehow managing to look vulnerable and provocative at the same time.

"Hello, Ethan."

"Hi." And, because no other words came to mind, he said simply, "Wow."

She smiled. Her vulnerability vanished. Sexy confidence took its place, dusting up his nerves.

"Wow to you too." Her gaze flicked down and she stepped forward. A pair of delicate hands skimmed down the lapels of his jacket. "Nice suit, Seaver."

"This old thing?" He shrugged. He was glad she hadn't seen him an hour ago, struggling to choose a shirt and tie and wondering if by showing up in his most expensive suit she would think he was trying too hard to impress her.

He helped her into her long wool coat, hiding a smile as she tucked away the price tag that had not yet been removed from one sleeve.

"I did a little shopping today," she admitted.

"Me, too." When her eyebrows rose in question, he said, "Shirt…and tie."

"You have good taste."

He helped her into his SUV, enjoying the way she wriggled on to the seat thanks to her slim-fitting skirt. "All set?"

She crossed her legs, adjusted her coat so that it covered her bare knees. "Yes."

As they drove he told her, "I made reservations at a restaurant in Sutton's Bay. It's a bit of a drive, but the food is excellent. The chef's specialty is a herb-crusted pork tenderloin."

"Sounds delicious."

And it was. The restaurant was small and exclusive, with reservations required and an ambitious waiting staff determined to make the guests' dining experience one to remember. Ethan had eaten there before, although never on a date. Now, as the lights were lowered and a string quartet began to play from a stage tucked into one corner, he watched Claire and felt swept away all over again. He wanted to blame his reaction to her on the room's romantic ambience or the glass of wine he'd consumed or even the daring plunge of her dress's neckline. But he knew it was the woman herself who'd tangled up his emotions. It was Claire who had tied up his heart.

Again.

He'd given up trying to figure out exactly how he felt

about that. Tonight he was just going to enjoy himself. And he did. He enjoyed the meal and the Pinot Noir that had been produced at a local winery. And he enjoyed her company, the give and take of their conversation and the way Claire gave him her undivided attention when he spoke.

After they left the restaurant, he took her arm and escorted her to his vehicle. Before opening the door for her, he kissed her soundly. "I want to make love to you, Claire."

He heard her breath hitch, but she replied, "I want that, too."

"I have guests at my house."

"We could go back to my room," she suggested and, though he couldn't see her face too clearly in the dim light from the moon, he thought she blushed. Vulnerable and provocative. It was a lethal combination.

"I've thought of that, but I'm not too keen on running into June on our way up the stairs."

"Neither am I. So where does that leave us?"

"Laura and James are leaving tomorrow afternoon and then…"

"We can be alone." She finished the thought for him.

They held hands on the way back to his SUV as well as on the long drive back to Glen Arbor. They didn't talk much, but the silence wasn't strained, even if it did hum with sexual tension. At the bed-and-breakfast, Ethan walked Claire to the front door as he had twice before. They stood under a halo of light from the porch's lamp and kissed good night like a couple of teenagers.

"This isn't quite how I imagined the evening ending," Ethan muttered.

"I thought it would end differently too," she admitted. "I shaved my legs. Put on sexy underwear."

"Don't tell me that now."

"Sorry."

He nodded, accepting her apology, but then he asked, "What color is it?"

"The underwear?"

"Uh-huh."

"Black."

He groaned. "I'm very fond of black. Do you have more in that color?"

On side of her mouth lifted. "I believe I do."

"Good. Wear it tomorrow." He kissed her quickly and then he was gone.

Claire stood on the porch and waited until the taillights of his vehicle had disappeared down the road before going inside. Tomorrow seemed an eternity away.

Claire rose early the next morning. She hadn't slept much. She'd been too keyed up to do much more than toss and turn. And to fantasize. Even so, she felt energized, excited. Ready.

She and Ethan had not spoken about love, but they had talked about starting over. Surely deep emotions were implied in such an endeavor. They were for Claire. Over the past few days she had begun to remember exactly why Ethan Seaver had caught her eye in the first place.

It hadn't been just his serious good looks or his independent streak, both of which she still found vastly appealing. No, it had been his teasing humor, his keen intellect, his basic kindness, sense of fair play and the way he'd made her feel special, important, capable. He still managed to do that, even though these days Claire no longer needed outside help to feel emboldened, to feel empowered.

Her ebullient mood lasted until she booted up her laptop and read the e-mail from the head of human resources at Mayfield. Stanley Robertson had sent her an overview of her severance package, no doubt at her father's request. Having spent more than a decade with the company, the letter noted that she was vested in its pension program and detailed the sum she would earn monthly once she reached retirement age. It was far less than she could live on comfortably, which wasn't really an issue since she had a sizable trust fund from which she could draw.

The letter went on to inform Claire that she would have to decide before the start of the new year what she wanted to do with her stock investment plan. She could cash out her tax-deferred savings at a significant penalty, or have them rolled over into an IRA account.

Finally, the e-mail instructed her that her final check, which included compensation for her unused vacation days, would not be released until she had turned in her name badge and the keys to her office. It concluded:

Any remaining personal effects on Mayfield premises will be disposed of if they have not been claimed by the end of the month.

The bluntly stated missive seemed so out of character for the kind man who had taken Claire under his wing when she'd first interned at Mayfield all those years earlier. But then, Sumner did sign Stanley's paychecks. Copies had been forwarded to her father and the law firm that the company kept on retainer.

"Gee, nothing in here about being disinherited," she mused aloud. "I guess that will come in a separate letter."

Claire closed the e-mail and turned off her computer. Sitting in the middle of the unmade bed, she rested her chin on her bent knees and sighed. She was sorry it had come to this, but not sorry she had stood firm, not sorry she had held her ground.

Ethan called just as she stepped out of the shower an hour later. She answered the telephone wrapped in a fluffy white towel, her short hair a wet spiky mess.

She had an inkling who it would be, so she said in her sexiest voice, "Good morning, handsome."

"You'd better be talking to me," he said with mock severity.

Claire grinned into the receiver and settled on the edge of the bed. "Who else?"

"So, how did you sleep?" he asked.

"How do you think?"

She heard him chuckle and pictured the corners of

his eyes crinkling with amusement. "I've got a pretty good idea."

She glanced at the clock on the nightstand. It was not quite ten a.m. "Is your…company already gone?"

He cleared his throat. "Yes. I suggested they leave early since freezing rain is forecast for later in the day."

Claire glanced outside at a nearly cloudless blue sky. "Really?"

"It could happen," he replied. "Michigan weather is never predictable."

She wasn't sure what to say in response, so she just made a little humming noise.

"Claire?"

"Yes?"

"How fast do you think you can get here?" he asked bluntly.

Her heart seemed to ricochet off her ribs, but she played it cool. "Well, if I were to borrow June's bike, it would take me about forty minutes since most of it is uphill."

"And if you were to take your car?"

"Oh, about fifteen once I get myself dressed and ready."

"Don't bother dressing and take the car."

She chuckled. "Okay."

She arrived in his driveway just half an hour after hanging up the telephone. This despite the fact that she'd had to blow-dry her hair, fuss with makeup and then change outfits three times before settling on a cashmere sweater in muted red that she'd paired with black pants and low-heeled boots.

Ethan was on the deck, arms crossed, legs braced apart as if he were standing on the bow of a wave-tossed ship. Their relationship certainly had known its share of rough seas, she mused. He was watching her. He was waiting for her. And, she realized she had been waiting for him. Any awkwardness she might have felt melted away as she closed the distance, dropped her purse on to one of the deck chairs. Their bodies bumped, molded through the layers of clothing, as she wound her arms around his neck and rose on tiptoe to greet him.

"Hi," she said after a long, long kiss.

His hands rubbed her back through her coat and sweater. "Hi."

"Let's go inside."

She followed him through the door. Other than his entryway the other day, she hadn't seen his home, but she wasn't interested in taking the grand tour now. She bypassed the firelit great room and headed up the stairs, glancing over her shoulder to ensure he was following her. He was. Stepping over the coat she'd tossed aside and the boots she'd shed.

"Last door on the left," he said, getting rid of his own shoes before peeling off his sweater.

She opened the door, glanced around briefly, before her gaze settled on the king-sized bed that dominated one wall. The comforter had been pulled up, the pillows neatly stacked against the headboard. She walked to it and sat on the edge of the mattress.

"You made your bed," she commented, running one palm over the down-filled cover. Then she held out her hand to him. "Let's mess it up again."

CHAPTER TEN

"IT'S FRIDAY," CLAIRE told Ethan.

"Thank God," came his heartfelt reply.

Unfortunately, the sentiments were offered via the telephone. She was back in Chicago and he was in Detroit.

Since their return from Glen Arbor a month earlier they had spent every weekend together either at his home or her apartment. During the week, when the miles stretched between them, they made do with daily phone calls, e-mails and text messages so racy they should have caused their cell phones to overheat.

If there was one blot on the horizon, it was that with Christmas just days away, Claire remained estranged from her parents. Even so, she had accepted that they might never come around to the fact that she had taken control of her own life. She was seriously involved with the man of her choosing and she'd begun to lay the ground work for a philanthropic foundation that would specialize in helping troubled families and children. She felt needed, necessary and complete.

"I was wondering what time you'll get in tonight," she asked Ethan. "I thought we could eat at my apartment. I have a dining room table now."

"That's a pity. I've enjoyed eating in your bed."

"We can still have dessert there."

"Have I told you how much I love the way you compromise?" Ethan replied. "In fact, I was hoping you might consider coming here for the weekend instead."

"I can do that," she said slowly. "Everything okay?"

"Fine, but I have a four o'clock meeting that I can't reschedule."

"You've had a lot of meetings lately. Have you found an investor?"

Ethan cleared his throat. "More or less."

He didn't sound pleased, but she let it go when he changed the subject. "I've got a couple of tickets for a show. Afterward we can grab a late dinner in Greektown."

"Not fair bribing me with baklava. How am I supposed to resist an offer like that?"

"You can't. That was my plan." He laughed. "I'll have a car meet you at the airport. Just call my secretary when you know your arrival time."

"Okay." She was alone in her apartment. Even so, she lowered her voice. "It's been a really long week, Ethan."

"Tell me about it." Then, "Want to make it a really long weekend?"

She mentally flipped through her day planner. "I have an appointment late Monday morning, but I could take the red-eye back."

"I was thinking you could stay through the middle of the week," he said. Then added, "Through Christmas."

Claire cleared her throat. Even so, her voice caught. "I…I thought you'd want to spend that with your family."

"I do. But I want you with me too." When she said nothing, he rushed ahead with, "Of course, I'll understand if you'd rather spend the holiday in Chicago with your parents."

Even if they had been on speaking terms, Claire knew what her answer would be. "I want to be with you, Ethan."

She didn't care where or who else would be present—her parents or his family. She wanted to spend Christmas with the man who had once been her husband and hopefully would be again. Which was why she'd reached a decision. First, she was going to tell him she loved him. They hadn't spoken the words aloud yet, although surely the meaning had been conveyed in so many other ways. Second, she was going to ask Ethan to marry her. It was only fitting that she do the honors. He'd asked the last time.

"I can't wait to see you," he said.

"Same here."

After Ethan hung up the phone he took a deep breath and expelled it. It wasn't nerves he felt, but anticipation. At some point during the past several weeks he'd stopped questioning his feelings for Claire. He'd stopped dwelling on what had gone wrong in their relationship before and started concentrating on what was right about it now.

It wasn't until after he'd accepted that Claire really had changed that he'd realized he had as well. Business remained important but, even as he moved ahead with expansion plans that would mean taking Seaver Security Solutions public after the first of the year, it was no longer his sole focus. Now, he wanted someone with whom he could share his life, his hopes and his dreams. Someone he could come home to after a long day and simply unwind with. He wanted that someone to be Claire.

He took a small velvet box from the drawer of his desk and flipped back the top. A large solitaire diamond set in platinum winked up at him.

A decade ago, he hadn't given Claire an engagement ring when he'd asked her to marry him. This time he would. He'd bought the matching wedding band. No cheap gold-plate this time. He planned to do everything right. This time, when he slipped it on her finger, he would do everything in his power to ensure she never had a reason to take it off.

"That's some sparkler, son."

The gravelly voice boomed in his office, causing Ethan's head to snap up. He could barely believe the sight that greeted his eyes. Sumner Mayfield stood at the door to his office.

Ethan closed the box and tucked it into one of the front pockets of his briefcase for safekeeping before rising to his feet.

"Sorry, Mr Seaver. He just walked right past me," Anita said.

"No problem," he told his worried secretary. "I've got a few minutes to spare for Mr. Mayfield. He and I are... old acquaintances."

When the door had closed behind them, Sumner said, "I assume I know the intended recipient of that ring. I'd heard you and Claire were seeing one another again. Not from my daughter, mind you. We're not on speaking terms, a fact that has left her mother devastated."

"Is that the reason for your unexpected visit this afternoon?" Ethan inquired.

"Actually, I'm here on business."

"I usually make appointments for that."

"Well, I hope you'll excuse my breach in etiquette since we are practically family," Sumner drawled.

"Again," Ethan added and had the pleasure of watching the older man scowl. "Please, have a seat."

Ethan was curious about the reason behind his once and hopefully future father-in-law's visit, but he'd long ago learned the value of keeping his emotions in check and his expression neutral when dealing with an adversary.

"You know," Sumner said, glancing around Ethan's tastefully appointed office, "I underestimated you, Seaver. You've done very well for yourself."

The compliment did nothing to lessen Ethan's apprehension. Indeed it had just the opposite effect. "You didn't think I was good enough for your daughter," he reminded Sumner.

"I still don't."

Ethan was more amused than insulted. "Only because you didn't handpick me. You've enjoyed running Claire's life. It must really tick you off that she's not letting you do it any longer."

A muscle jumped in the older man's cheek, the only sign that Ethan's words had had any effect. "Let's get down to business."

"I hope this won't take long." Ethan glanced at his watch. "I have another meeting in an hour."

"I'll keep it brief." Sumner offered a sharklike smile. "I understand from certain sources that Seaver Security Solutions is going to have a public stock offering at some point in the coming year."

Ethan shrugged dismissively, even though he felt gut-punched. How did the older man know that? He'd shared the details with no one outside of a few key executives at Seaver, and the lawyers and investment bankers of course. He'd been careful to keep a closed lid on things so as not to be accused of violating the Securities Act that forbade public offering discussions before an IPO was registered with the Security Exchange Commission.

"I don't know what you're talking about."

Sumner chuckled. "Come now, son. I have it on good authority that the SEC has approved your prospectus." The document was needed to initiate the offering of a company's stock. "Once the share price is finalized you'll be good to go."

Denying it again seemed pointless, so Ethan said, "That's not public knowledge."

"Which is why I'm here." Sumner's smile would have done Lucifer proud and it made Ethan just as uneasy. "I've heard that you have a patented security system that you're eager to move into production. That takes money."

"Hence the IPO," Ethan replied, trying to appear bored even as his nerves were snapping. "And, if you're hoping to get in the ground floor, I have to warn you the SEC frowns on discussing a public offering before an IPO is officially registered."

"So that's the route you're determined to take?" Sumner asked. "I'd heard you were hoping to find an investor."

Ethan merely shrugged. "Changed my mind."

"Well, there are a lot of advantages to a publicly held company. I can attest to that firsthand as the head of Mayfield. There's also a downside." Sumner leaned forward. "The company you've sweated to build from nothing won't be solely yours any longer. You'll have shareholders to answer to, paperwork to fill out and hell to pay when a quarter's earnings aren't what investors feel they should have been."

He'd just listed Ethan's biggest concerns. "Let's cut to the chase. Why are you here, Sumner?"

"I'm offering you a mutually advantageous alternative." The older man pulled out a manila folder, which he pushed across the desk to Ethan.

After opening it, Ethan glanced up. "This is a contract."

"I'm interested in becoming a partner, a silent partner. After five years you can buy me out for the same amount of my investment—no interest, no penalty. It's an incredibly generous offer."

Ethan snorted. "Let me guess the conditions."

"There's only one."

"Claire."

Sumner nodded. "See, you are bright, son."

"Don't call me son," Ethan said evenly. He pushed the folder back across the desk and stood. "I don't want your money and I certainly don't want you as my partner, silent or otherwise. I'll settle for you as my father-in-law, but only because I have to." He shook his head, angry and hurt on Claire's behalf. "Your daughter is incredible. She is bright and interesting and far smarter than you give her credit for. You insult not only me but her with this offer."

Sumner rose on a curse. "You're a fool!"

"No, sir. You're the fool for thinking you could buy me off. I love Claire. And that's the only reason I'm not calling security right now to have you escorted from the building."

"You'll regret this," Sumner warned.

"No. I won't."

When Sumner had gone, Ethan slumped back into his chair. He reached for the contract which the older man had left on the desktop. Flipping open the folder, he eyed the offer again. Sumner had certainly sweetened the deal since the last time he'd tried to buy off Ethan. Poor Claire. What was he going to tell her? As Ethan stuffed the folder into his briefcase, he decided any mention of this matter could wait. What was the point in ruining her holiday with this news?

The day before Christmas found Ethan and Claire enjoying an intimate dinner at his home. Ethan's mother, his brothers, their wives and children, including the newest baby, who had been born the week before, would gather together around the nine-foot-tall Douglas fir in his vaulted great room the following afternoon. This evening, however, Claire had him all to herself. She planned to make the most of their time alone.

To start, she'd decided to cook for him. In Chicago, she'd relied on an excellent caterer for their meals or simple dishes she could prepare herself. Not this time. She'd spent the better part of the morning scouring Web sites for recipes before setting out in the afternoon to purchase the necessary ingredients. She would be making coq au vin, rosemary-roasted red potatoes and a Caesar salad. They would finish the meal with praline chocolate crème brûlée.

It was an ambitious menu given her very limited culinary skills, but Claire felt up to the challenge…until it was time to serve it. She'd wanted the meal to be memorable and she got her wish, which was why at seven o'clock they were awaiting the delivery of a pizza.

"I'm really sorry about dinner," she said. The under-cooked potatoes had already been tossed down the disposal and the odor of charred meat was dissipating thanks to the cold breeze blowing through the opened kitchen windows. Dessert was a failure, too. Only the salad remained edible.

"It's okay. I like pizza." Ethan wisely tucked away his smile.

"It was the thought that counts," she muttered.

"Then why don't you show me how thoughtful you can be?" he suggested in a silky voice and the intense way in which he regarded her raised gooseflesh on her arms.

"Right now?"

"Why not? No time like the present," he replied.

"Okay. Consider this the appetizer." She walked to him, tugging off a white chef's apron as she went. Next came her blouse, which she took her time unbuttoning. The skirt was last. When she stood before him, wearing only strategically placed scraps of silk and lace, she raised her eyebrows. "I think you're overdressed for the occasion."

"I'd have to agree," he said, reaching up to yank his sweater over his head.

"Here, let me help." When she had divested him of his pants they stumbled together toward the hallway.

"Bedroom's too damned far away," Ethan murmured against her lips and guided her backward through the door to the den.

They were still lying in a languid heap on the cushions of the couch when the doorbell rang twenty minutes later.

"Pizza," Claire mustered up the strength to whisper.

"Thank goodness it wasn't here in the promised thirty minutes or less."

Ethan laughed and rolled off her, knocking his briefcase from the corner of his desk as he stumbled about in the darkened room.

"Where on earth are my pants?" he grunted. The doorbell pealed a second time.

Claire giggled, but reached over to flip on the floor lamp. "Kitchen, remember. Next to my skirt, I believe."

"Right." He muttered a curse before going off in search of his clothing.

Claire didn't feel like moving, but she was cold now that Ethan's warm body had been removed, so she sat up and pulled the chenille throw from the back of the couch. She spied Ethan's briefcase, which he'd knocked over when he'd left the room and was now lying on its side, papers spilling out on to the floor, and so she bent down to gather them up. She intended only to stuff them back into the case, but a name on the top paper caught her eye.

Sumner Mayfield.

It was a contract, she realized, and began flipping frantically through the pages while her heart pounded. Her father was offering to become a silent partner in Ethan's company. The amount of the buy-in was substantial. Ethan's expansion plans certainly could move ahead. Why would her father do that? And why hadn't Ethan said anything?

She recalled their telephone conversation from the

other day. She'd asked then if he'd found an investor. What was it he'd said? *More or less.* He hadn't sounded pleased. Or maybe he'd sounded…guilty?

When she heard footsteps coming down the hallway, Claire stuffed the papers back into the briefcase. Ethan was at the doorway when she got to her feet.

Ask him about the contract, she told herself. But she didn't. She needed him to tell her.

"Dinner is served," he announced with an exaggerated bow. He held the pizza box aloft on one hand and might have made a credible waiter except that he was shirtless, shoeless and the top button on his trousers remained undone.

They ate at the table in the dining room. Claire served the Caesar salad with the pizza. A good bottle of wine and a couple of lighted candles nudged the meal to the passable range.

"You're awfully quiet," Ethan noted. She seemed distracted and not necessarily in a good way. It made him uneasy. "Something on your mind?"

Claire nodded. She picked up her wineglass and sipped, as if seeking courage. Then she said, "I…I saw what was in your briefcase, Ethan. I wasn't spying. You knocked it over when you went to answer the door, remember? The contents spilled out on to the floor. It was just there…in front of me. "

"I should have put it in a better hiding place, I guess," he said, thinking of the engagement ring.

He watched her swallow. She seemed oddly disappointed when she asked, "So, you didn't want me to see it?"

"No. I mean, not yet. Not until I'd asked you a very important question and gotten your answer."

"What question?" she whispered.

Ethan wiped her mouth on his napkin and set it aside. This wasn't going at all according to plan. There was nothing remotely romantic about the moment. Still, he rose from his seat and came around the table.

"I know things are moving fast," he said, taking Claire's hand in his. Her fingers felt like ice. "That seems to be the only speed the two of us know.

"Ethan—" She shook her head.

But he forged ahead. "I love you, Claire. I don't think I ever stopped loving you. And I want to make a life with you. Will you marry me? Again."

Her eyes blurred with tears, but he didn't get the feeling they were happy ones, even when she said, "I love you too."

Ethan swallowed. "Why do I have a bad feeling there's a but coming?"

A tear leaked down her cheek. "Tell me, because I need to know. Will…will what's in your briefcase be returned if my answer is no?"

Dread pooled in his stomach. He recalled that when Claire had returned the wedding band she'd told him that she'd decided she couldn't keep it because it had represented a promise. Well, no promises had been made this time. Ethan shook his head. "No. It won't be returned, no matter what your answer is. It's a gift, Claire."

"You consider it a gift?"

He frowned. "Yes."

"How can you consider it a gift?" Her voice rose. "That's several million dollars we're talking about!"

"Claire, I know the diamond is several carats, but it's not worth millions," he told her.

"Diamond?" She blinked.

Ethan rubbed the back of his neck. "I get the feeling we're talking about two different things."

"I saw my father's offer."

"The contract." He swore.

"Yes. He wants to invest in your company. When exactly did that come about?"

"A few days ago. Sumner came to my office unannounced and just sprang it on me."

"And you didn't see fit to tell me?" she asked.

"I didn't want to upset you. It's Christmas, but I planned to talk to you about it eventually."

"What did you tell my father?"

The question left him feeling mule-kicked. "I told him no, Claire. You have to ask?"

"I'm sorry," she said, but she didn't exactly appear apologetic.

"I'm sorry too," he spat. "I thought you trusted me."

She swallowed. "And I thought you considered me an adult."

"What's that supposed to mean? Of course I consider you an adult."

"No, you don't. You can't." She shook her head as her eyes filled. "Or you would have told me about my father's visit right away."

"Claire." He reached for her hand. "Don't cry, sweetheart. I didn't tell you because I didn't want to see you upset like you are right now."

She yanked her hand free and stood, tossing down the napkin that had been on her lap. "Don't! Don't do that!" she shouted. "Don't treat me like I'm a damned child in need of coddling and protection. I won't allow my parents to do that any longer. What makes you think I will allow you to do it now?"

He stepped back and gave his own anger rein. "Well, excuse me for trying to spare your feelings."

"They don't need sparing!" she shouted. "I'm a big girl. I can take it!"

"Fine. Then here it is. Your father offered to become a silent partner in Seaver, allowing me to buy him out after five years, as long as I agreed to end things with you now."

A tear slipped down her cheek. "I can't believe he tried that again."

Ethan swallowed. "And I can't believe you'd think, even for a minute, that I'd be interested in taking anything from your father. You should know me better than that."

"I should," she agreed. "And you should know me better too. I deserve your honesty."

"I deserve your trust."

They eyed one another stoically for several minutes. Ethan was the first to break the silence.

"So, what now?"

Claire tipped up her chin. Mad and hurt as she was, she wasn't planning to give up without a fight. Not this time. "Are you asking if I need a ride to the airport?"

"No, because I won't take you. If you want to walk out on me, Claire, you'll have to call a cab."

She folded her arms across her chest. "Well, it's a good thing I don't want to leave."

"You don't?"

She studied his expression. Was that relief?

"No. This time I'm staying," she said. And her heart soared because he definitely looked relieved. Then she tilted her head to one side and asked, "But if I had decided to go, would you have come after me?"

Ethan snorted. "You bet I would have. I'm not making that mistake twice."

"Good," she said.

Ethan echoed the sentiment. Then he asked, "So, are you still mad?"

"You'd better believe it." She nodded for emphasis. "And you?"

"Yep. Royally ticked off."

Claire picked up the napkin she'd tossed on to the seat of her chair. "Well, then, let's sit back down and talk this out."

"Like adults," he said.

She allowed a brief smile to bow her lips. "Yes, like adults."

The discussion lasted the better part of an hour, during which they each made their feelings plainly known. Ethan promised to tell Claire everything in the future, even if it was news that was sure to upset her. Claire promised to trust Ethan completely and talk about her concerns openly to prevent misunderstandings.

They moved to the bedroom for the making up part. Afterward, with Claire lying snug in his arms, Ethan said, "There's still one thing I need to know."

"Anything," she murmured.

"I asked you a question earlier. You never answered it. So I'm going to ask again." He levered himself up on one elbow so he could see her face. "Will you—"

Claire stopped his words with her hand and scooted into a sitting position. "Wait. I want to do the proposing this time. I had it all planned, even if I didn't buy a ring."

Ethan pulled her hand aside so he could speak. "You were going to propose to *me?*"

She grinned. "Well, it seemed only fitting. You got to do it the first time, after all."

"Actually, I'm two up on you now," he pointed out, but he was grinning too.

Claire felt her heart bump against her ribs as she gave voice to the words that would complete a journey she'd begun so long ago. "I love you, Ethan Seaver. I'll never love anyone else. I want to marry you. I want to have a family with you. I want to be your best friend and your lover for the rest of my life."

He whistled through his teeth. "Wow. That's some proposal."

"I've been practicing it in front of the mirror for the past week," she admitted.

"Really? I was just going to wing it with mine."

"I'm no good at extemporaneous speaking." She shifted on to her knees. "Well?" she said impatiently.

He pulled her down on top of him and kissed her deeply.

Afterward, she asked in a breathless whisper, "Is that your answer?"

Ethan smiled. "That's my answer. Can you figure it out or do you need a translation? I don't want there to be any more miscommunication between us."

Claire smiled back. "I think I've figured it out." Leaning down for another kiss, she said, "But why don't you tell me again just to be sure?"

"Glad to." And he did.

EPILOGUE

CLAIRE STOOD WITH Belle and Simone in the same spot
high in the Himalayas where the three women had made
their pact a year earlier. They'd been looking back then,
retracing the miles they'd traveled, and eager to alter the
courses of their futures.

And they had.

Now they were facing forward—three strong, independent and capable women who had reached deep
inside themselves and discovered the courage to determine their destinies.

"So much has happened in a year," Claire mused.

"I know," Simone said.

"If one of you had told me I'd be a mother now, I'd
have thought you insane," Belle added. She and Ivo had
welcomed a daughter in August. Even so, she'd insisted
on making their reunion trip. And already she looked incredible. Of course.

"Well, what do you think?" Simone asked. "Should
we keep going?"

"Nah." Claire lowered the kickstand on her bike and removed her helmet. "I think we should stop, wait."

The other women dismounted their bikes as well. Together they turned and looked back down the trail. Three riders were approaching, their progress slow after such a long and challenging day.

"Ryan looks tired," Simone mused as she waved to her new husband.

"Ivo as well," Belle agreed, blowing a kiss to the man in question.

Claire watched Ethan and felt the pressure building in her chest as he grew closer. His gaze was locked on hers. His smile was full of promise. They'd been married nearly six months now, living together in his home in Detroit, and she remained blissfully happy and plenty busy with her new foundation. Ethan was busy as well. His company had gone public four months earlier. Knowing his mixed feelings on the endeavor, Claire had asked him to let her invest in the company instead so that it could remain privately held. She'd been considering it anyway, but he'd declined the offer. She hadn't taken no for an answer, though. She'd merely bided her time. When the IPO was announced, she'd made her move. She was now the largest shareholder in the publicly traded Seaver Security Solutions.

"They've come a long way," Belle said just before the men arrived.

Claire reached for her friends' hands. "I'd say we all have."

HARLEQUIN Romance.

New York Times bestselling author

DIANA PALMER

Handsome, eligible ranch owner Stuart York knew
Ivy Conley was too young for him, so he closed his heart
to her and sent her away—despite the fireworks between
them. Now, years later, Ivy is determined not to be
treated like a little girl anymore…but for some reason,
Stuart is always fighting her battles for her. And safe in
Stuart's arms makes Ivy feel like a woman…his woman.

Winter Roses

Available November.

HRIBC03985

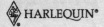

REQUEST YOUR FREE BOOKS!
2 FREE NOVELS PLUS 2
FREE GIFTS!

From the Heart, For the Heart

HR07

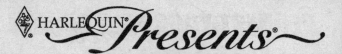

Always passionate, always proud.

**The richest royal family in the world—
a family united by blood and passion,
torn apart by deceit and desire.**

Don't miss

THE TYCOON'S
PRINCESS BRIDE

by favorite Harlequin Romance author

Natasha Oakley!

Isabella can't be in the same room as Domenic Vincini
without wanting him! But if she gives in to temptation
she forfeits her chance of being queen...and will tie
Niroli to its sworn enemy!

This sparkling story is part of the fabulous
Royal House of Niroli series—available in
Harlequin Presents this month!

Available October wherever you buy books!

HARLEQUIN *Romance*.

Coming Next Month

Fall in love with our ranchers, bosses and single dads in a month filled with mistletoe and magic, and where happy endings are guaranteed!

#3985 WINTER ROSES Diana Palmer
Long, Tall Texans

Rugged rancher Stuart has always been protective of innocent Ivy. Growing up and finding your place in the world is tough, but there's nowhere Ivy feels more like a woman than in Stuart's arms. A fantastic new book from an award-winning author.

#3986 THE COWBOY'S CHRISTMAS PROPOSAL Judy Christenberry
Mistletoe & Marriage

The first book in this festive duet that's sure to get you in the Christmas mood. Penny has just inherited her family ranch, but she has a problem... she doesn't know how to run it! Luckily, help is at hand in the form of Jake, the gorgeous cowboy next door....

#3987 APPOINTMENT AT THE ALTAR Jessica Hart
Bridegroom Boss

Free spirit Lucy doesn't like being told what to do, so when irresistible tycoon Guy challenges her to find a real job, she does—as Guy's assistant! Don't miss the second book in this wonderful duet.

#3988 THE BOSS'S DOUBLE TROUBLE TWINS Raye Morgan
9 to 5

Don't you just love surprises? Workaholic businessman Mitch gets a big one when new employee and old flame Darcy gives him news that will change his life—he's going to be a daddy, to twins!

#3989 CARING FOR HIS BABY Caroline Anderson
Heart to Heart

Everyone makes mistakes, and sometimes second chances can be even sweeter than the first time around. When Emily opens her door to Harry, the man who broke her heart years before, he is cradling a little baby in his arms. How can she resist?

#3990 MIRACLE ON CHRISTMAS EVE Shirley Jump

If you love this joyful season, don't miss single father C.J. struggling with newfound fatherhood, and yearning for a magical Christmas. Jessica's heart is quickly won by C.J.'s enchanting daughter, but what about the man himself?

HRCNM1007